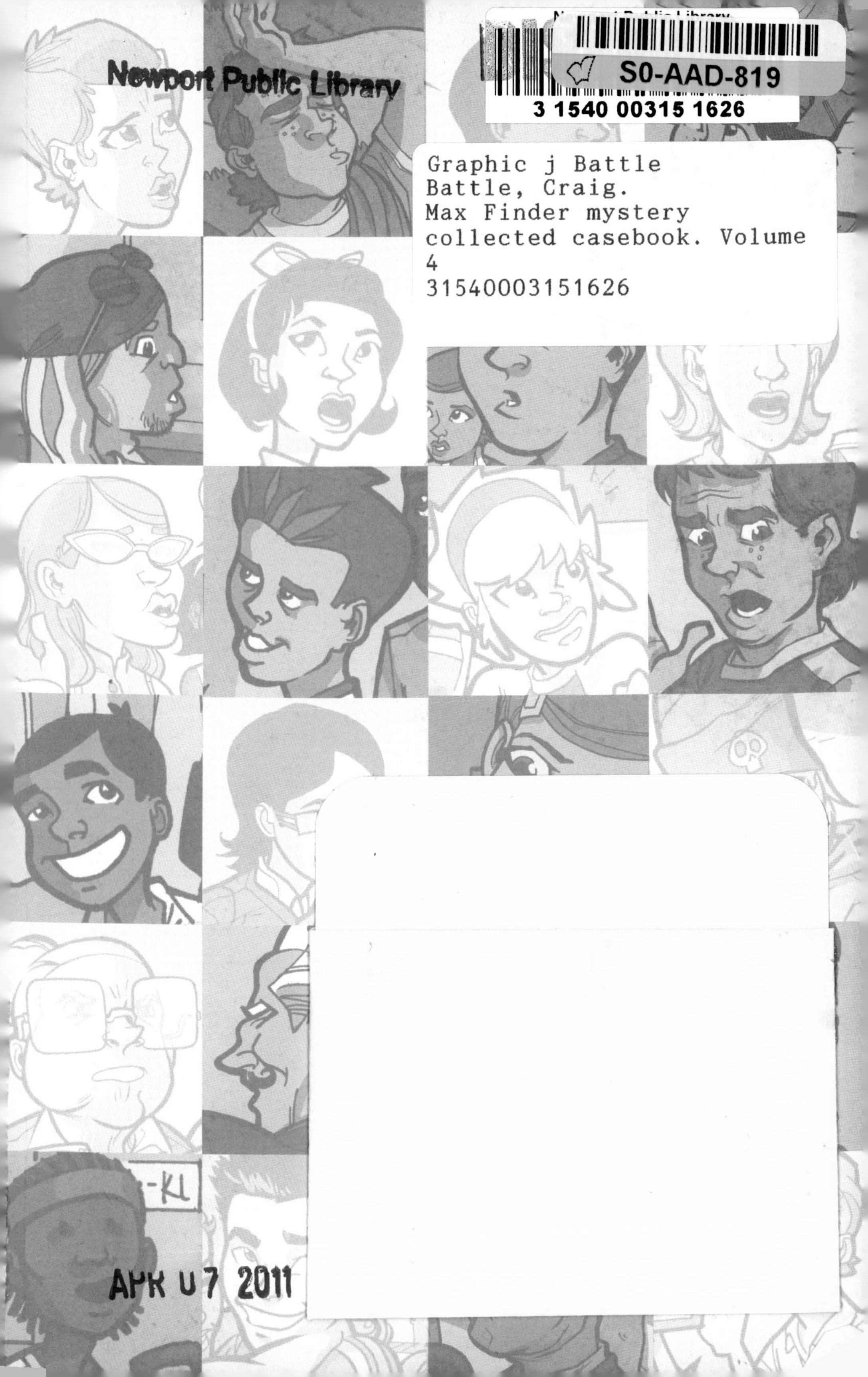

ALSO IN THE SERIES

Max Finder Mystery Collected Casebook, Volume 1
2007 Winner for Graphic Novel,
The Association of Educational Publishers'
Distinguished Achievement Award

Max Finder Mystery Collected Casebook, Volume 2
2008 Winner for Graphic Novel,
The Association of Educational Publishers'
Distinguished Achievement Award

Max Finder Mystery Collected Casebook, Volume 3
2008 Finalist for Graphic Novel,
The Association of Educational Publishers'
Distinguished Achievement Award

Max Finder

MYSTERY
Collected Casebook

Volume 4

© 2010 Owlkids Books Inc.
10 Lower Spadina Avenue, Suite 400, Toronto, Ontario M5V 2Z2
www.owlkids.com

Text © 2009 Liam O'Donnell (The Case of the Game Card Grab, The Case of the Haunted Babysitter, The Case of the Snatched Skateboard)
Additional illustrations by Scott Hepburn (pages 31, 34, 47, 50, 69, 72)

Distributed in Canada by Raincoast Books
9050 Shaughnessy Street, Vancouver, British Columbia V6P 6E5

Distributed in the United States by Publishers Group West
1700 Fourth Street, Berkeley, California 94710

Library and Archives Canada Cataloguing in Publication

O'Donnell, Liam, 1970-
      Max Finder mystery : collected casebook / Liam O'Donnell, Michael Cho.

Vol. 4. by Liam O'Donnell, Craig Battle, Ramón Pérez.
ISBN 2-89579-116-3 (v. 1).--ISBN 978-2-89579-116-4 (v. 1).--
ISBN 978-2-89579-121-8 (v. 2).--ISBN 978-2-89579-149-2 (v. 3).--
ISBN 978-1-897349-80-9 (v. 4)

      1. Detective and mystery comic books, strips, etc.--Juvenile fiction.
2. Mystery games--Juvenile fiction. I. Cho, Michael II. Battle, Craig, 1980-
III. Pérez, Ramón IV. Title.

PN6733.O36M38 2006   j741.5'971   C2006-903300-5

Library of Congress Control Number: 2009935531

Series Design: John Lightfoot/Lightfoot Art & Design Inc.
Design and Art Direction: Susan Sinclair

Canada Council for the Arts **Conseil des Arts du Canada** **ONTARIO ARTS COUNCIL** **CONSEIL DES ARTS DE L'ONTARIO**

We acknowledge the financial support of the Canada Council for the Arts, the Ontario Arts Council, the Government of Canada through the Book Publishing Industry Development Program (BPIDP), and the Government of Ontario through the Ontario Media Development Corporation's Book Initiative for our publishing activities.

Manufactured by Sheck Wah Tong Printing Press Ltd
Manufactured in Guang Dong, China in December 2009
Job #46228

A   B   C   D   E   F

 Publisher of Chirp, chickaDEE and OWL
www.owlkids.com

Max Finder

MYSTERY

Collected Casebook

Volume 4

Craig Battle and Ramón Pérez

Created by Liam O'Donnell

Max Finder
MYSTERY
Collected Casebook

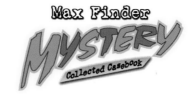

Contents

Stories

Extra Stuff

Collected
Casebook
Volume 4

HEY MYSTERY BUFFS!

Did you know that the book in your hands features a whopping ten comics and three stories? Max Finder here, fact collector and junior high detective. My best friend Alison and I investigate all sorts of mysteries in our hometown of Whispering Meadows, and many of our finest moments are collected for you right here.

From the **Disappearing Painting** to the **Pinched Pooch**, each mystery is crammed with enough clues, suspects, and red herrings to keep you guessing until the end. We've done all the legwork, but solving the mystery is up to you! Read the mysteries, watch for clues, and try to crack the case. Solutions are at the end of each comic. But remember: real detectives never peek.

So fire up your mystery radar and get solving!

Max

P.S. Check out the character files starting on page 11!

Meet the Characters

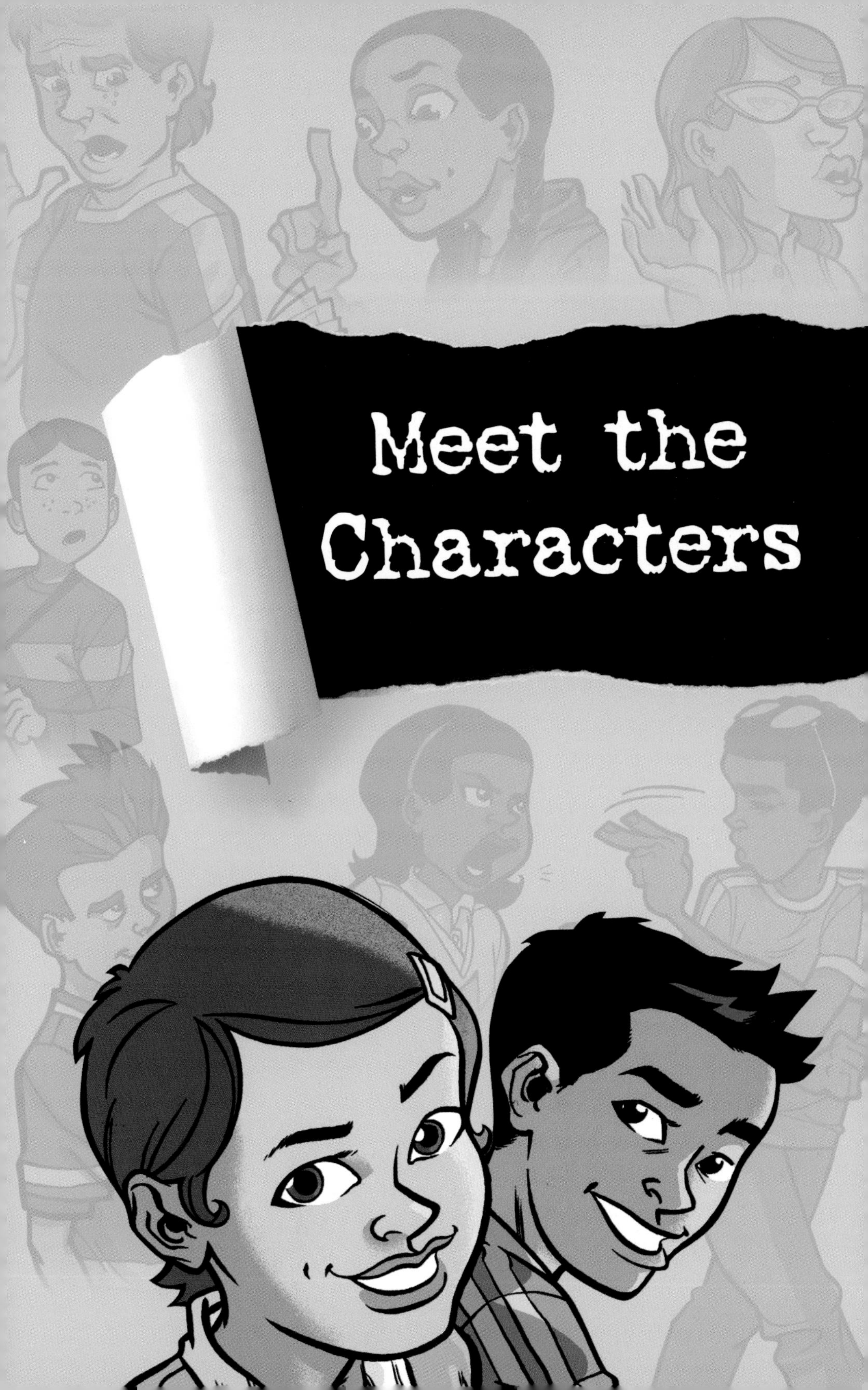

Max Finder

Max has a nose for mysteries and a brain for unusual facts. Like his hero, Sherlock Holmes, 12-year-old Max uses logic and observation to solve mysteries in his hometown of Whispering Meadows. In his leisure time, Max likes to read detective novels, ride his skateboard, avoid his chores, and stake out crime scenes with his best friend, Alison.

Alison Santos

Friends since kindergarten, Alison and Max share a passion for mysteries. An aspiring journalist, Alison has an insatiable taste for adventure and a desire to uncover the truth. Max and Alison are a real team, as she likes to remind Max, "If it wasn't for me, you'd still be finding lost marbles for the kids in daycare."

LOST DOG

VERY FRIENDLY, ANSWERS TO PEACHES. PLEASE CALL

Zoe Palgrave

Zoe is a chip off the old block. Her mom is a forensics crime scene investigator, and though Zoe is only 11, she's already following in her mom's footsteps. Zoe's scientific skills and knowledge — not to mention her basement laboratory — have helped Max and Alison solve many cases.

Leslie Chang

Leslie is the ultimate high achiever, dedicated organizer, and tireless busybody with a juicy piece of gossip on every student and teacher at school. She's a great source of information for Max and Alison, except when she is a suspect herself.

Tony DeMatteo

Tony is an all-around athlete. He plays football and is the captain of the hockey team. This jock also has a sensitive side and cries at sad movies.

Jake Granger

If Jake and Max didn't dislike each other so much, they might be best friends. That's because Jake loves mysteries nearly as much as Max does. He's also a fan of magic and the paranormal, and often isn't too far from any Whispering Meadows crime scene.

Ben "Basher" McGintley

With fists the size of pumpkins, 14-year-old Basher is always looking for fresh stomachs to punch. Basher's scowls and grunts often hide key clues for Max and Alison.

Nanda Kanwar

Nanda always has the latest CDs and clothes. This hockey goaltender would not hesitate to pass blame on a friend if it kept her out of trouble.

Kyle Kressman

Kyle is a practical joker at heart — and at school. He's a master of stink bombs and whoopee cushions, and is easygoing to the max — except when the joke's on him.

Sasha Price

Sasha's family lives on an estate outside Whispering Meadows. She's not always considerate of others, and especially not her neighbor, Nicholas Musicco.

Nicholas Musicco

Nicholas is small for his age and not very athletic. He's well-spoken, confident, and possesses a very sharp mind.

Jessica Peeves

Seeing as her dad is the mayor of Whispering Meadows, Jessica is the town's "first daughter." To the chagrin of her classmates, she's a natural at just about everything she tries.

Alex Rodriguez

Alex strives to be number one at everything — especially chess. Aged 12, he hopes to be a millionaire within the next ten years. He's always dressed for success.

Josh "Rumbler" Spodek

Known simply as "Rumbler" because of his deep voice, Josh loves fishing and sports. He's known for his easy-going nature — until you get on his bad side.

Leo Ducharme

Leo flies under the radar at Central Meadows Junior High — and likes it that way. He looks younger than his 13 years, loves computers, and has several hobbies.

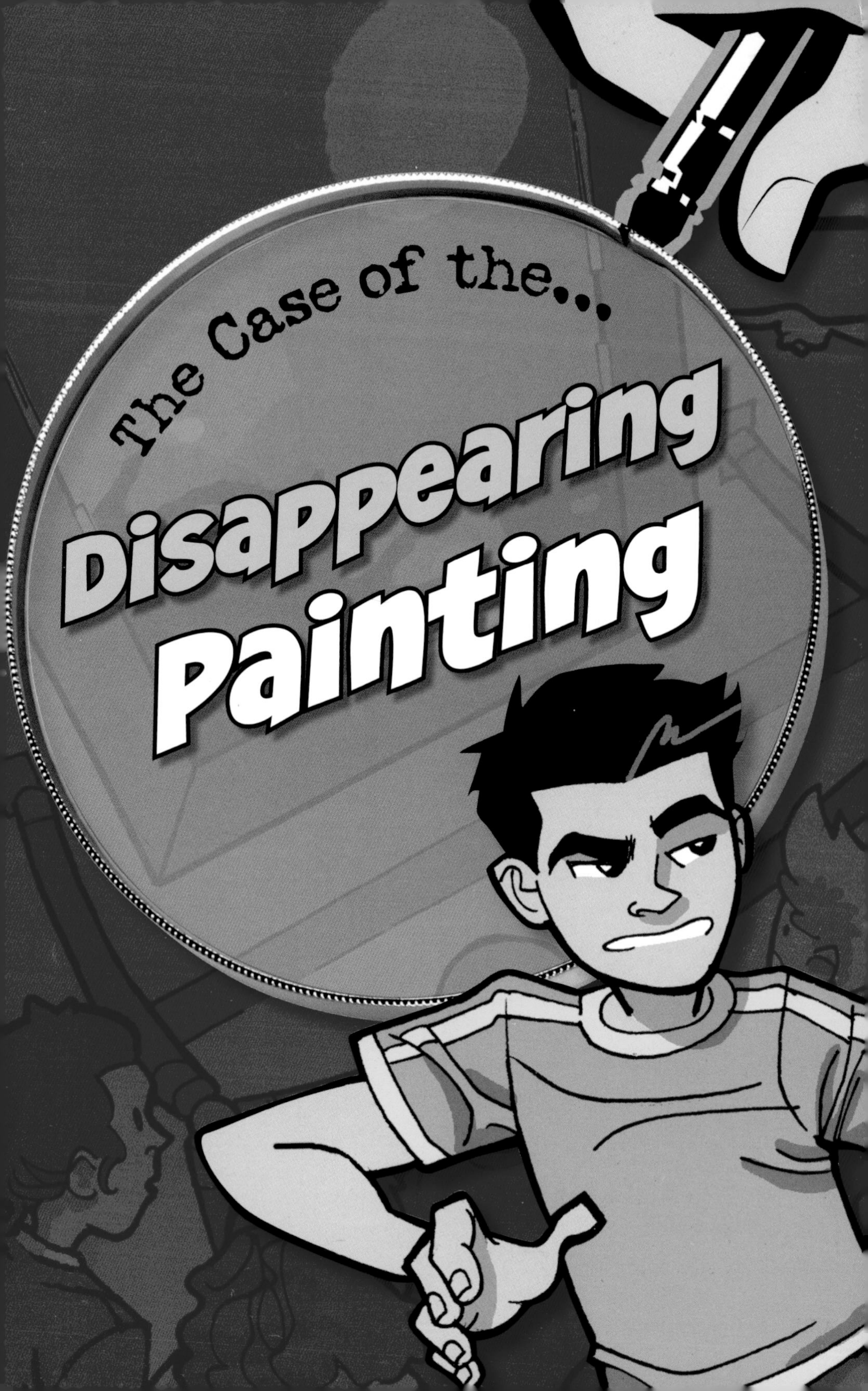
The Case of the...
Disappearing
Painting

The Case of the Disappearing Painting

First week back and already a field trip? Sounds like my kind of school year. Max Finder, junior high detective, here. My class was at the museum to check out the unveiling of Whispering Meadows' most famous painting.

ARE YOU AN ART LOVER, MAX?

I DON'T KNOW, ALISON. DO THE COVERS OF SHERLOCK HOLMES BOOKS COUNT?

Our classmate Layne Jennings is a huge art fan — and a pretty good artist herself.

I CAN'T WAIT TO SEE THIS PAINTING! I'VE ONLY SEEN IT IN BOOKS BECAUSE IT'S BEEN IN A PRIVATE COLLECTION.

ONE MOMENT by EMMELINE PARR

The painting, *One Moment* by Emmeline Parr, normally hangs in Mayor Peeves's mansion. But since he decided to auction it, the town's been buzzing.

STUDENTS, WE'RE NOT THE ONLY ONES HERE TODAY. THERE ARE JOURNALISTS, ART BUYERS, AND OTHER ARTISTS AROUND, SO BE ON YOUR BEST BEHAVIOR.

EMPLOYEES ONLY

MR. REED WASN'T KIDDING. THERE'S VICTOR PRICE, THE AUCTIONEER.

AND MARJORY PARR. SHE'S A DIRECT DESCENDANT OF EMMELINE PARR.

Finally! The show was on the road. Unfortunately, it wasn't the show we'd been promised.

THAT'S NOT THE PAINTING. THAT'S A FAKE!

Museum staff confirmed Layne's fears: the real painting was missing. Wild rumors started to spread like wildfire.

THIS DOESN'T LOOK GOOD FOR MAYOR PEEVES. I WONDER HOW JESSICA IS TAKING IT...

HEY, CHIEF, I'VE GOT A WEB EXCLUSIVE: PEEVES TRIED TO AUCTION OFF A COUNTERFEIT. HE'S GOING FROM POLITICIAN TO PRISONER!

MAX!

Sometimes having a reputation as a good detective is more trouble than it's worth. Jessica is Mayor Peeves's daughter — and our school's resident prima donna.

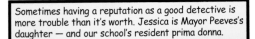

I SAW THE REAL PAINTING HANGING HERE THIS MORNING, SO IT MUST STILL BE IN THE BUILDING. IF IT GETS OUTSIDE, MY DAD IS IN TROUBLE. AND IF MY DAD IS IN TROUBLE...

SO IS MAX. WE GET IT, JESSICA.

HMM, WHAT DO YOU GUYS THINK?

IF MAYOR PEEVES IS A COUNTERFEITER, HE'S THE WORST ONE IN THE WORLD.

IT LOOKS LIKE THE REAL PAINTING WAS CUT OUT OF THE FRAME WITH A KNIFE.

AND THIS CRUMMY COPY WAS STUCK ON WITH SCOTCH TAPE.

THE PAINTING IS OBVIOUSLY A FAKE. IT MUST'VE BEEN MEANT TO DISTRACT US WHILE THE THIEF WALKED OFF WITH THE REAL MCCOY.

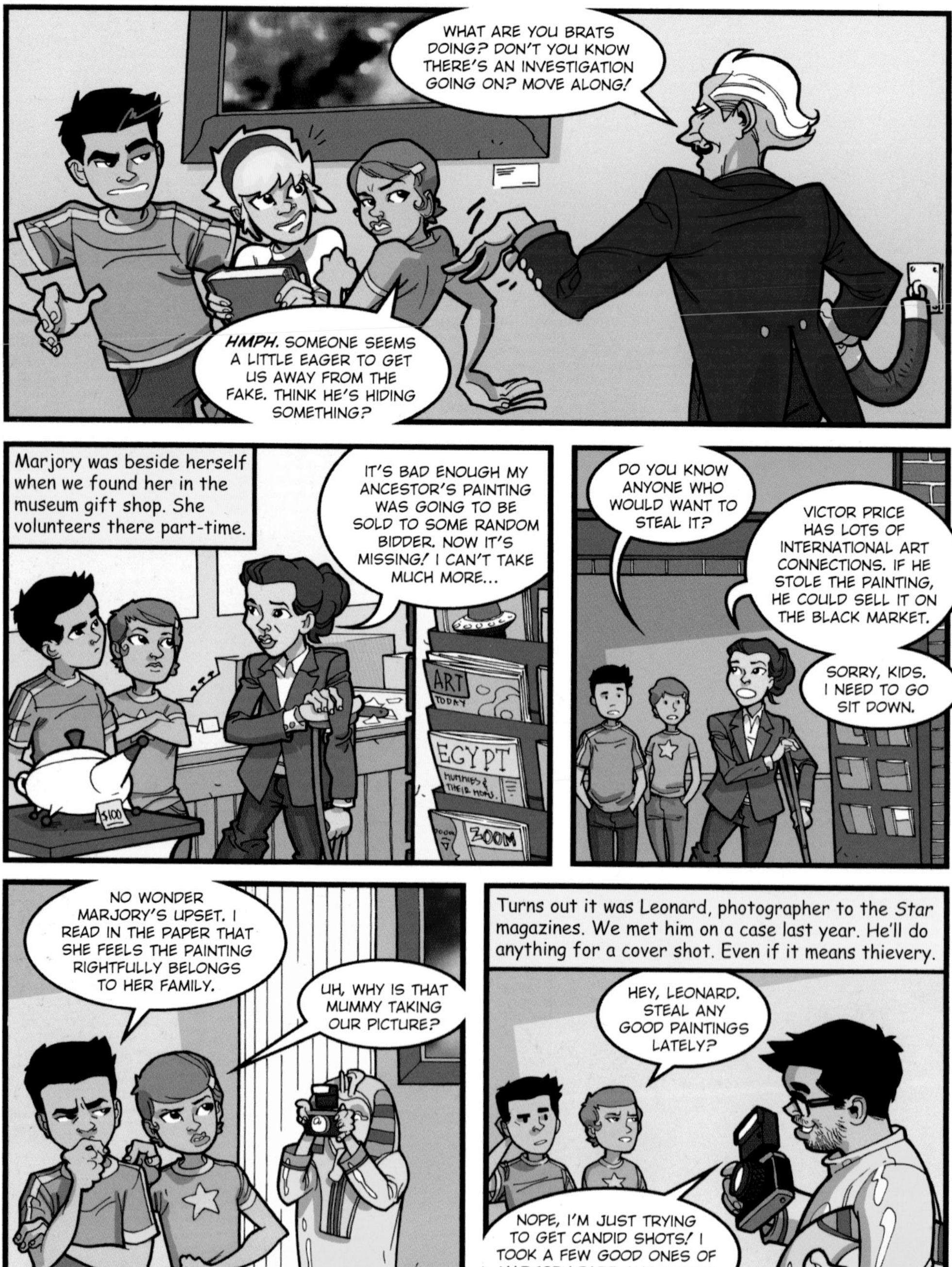
WHAT ARE YOU BRATS DOING? DON'T YOU KNOW THERE'S AN INVESTIGATION GOING ON? MOVE ALONG!
HMPH. SOMEONE SEEMS A LITTLE EAGER TO GET US AWAY FROM THE FAKE. THINK HE'S HIDING SOMETHING?
Marjory was beside herself when we found her in the museum gift shop. She volunteers there part-time.
IT'S BAD ENOUGH MY ANCESTOR'S PAINTING WAS GOING TO BE SOLD TO SOME RANDOM BIDDER. NOW IT'S MISSING! I CAN'T TAKE MUCH MORE...
ART TODAY
EGYPT
ZOOM
$100
DO YOU KNOW ANYONE WHO WOULD WANT TO STEAL IT?
VICTOR PRICE HAS LOTS OF INTERNATIONAL ART CONNECTIONS. IF HE STOLE THE PAINTING, HE COULD SELL IT ON THE BLACK MARKET.
SORRY, KIDS. I NEED TO GO SIT DOWN.
NO WONDER MARJORY'S UPSET. I READ IN THE PAPER THAT SHE FEELS THE PAINTING RIGHTFULLY BELONGS TO HER FAMILY.
UH, WHY IS THAT MUMMY TAKING OUR PICTURE?
Turns out it was Leonard, photographer to the Star magazines. We met him on a case last year. He'll do anything for a cover shot. Even if it means thievery.
HEY, LEONARD. STEAL ANY GOOD PAINTINGS LATELY?
NOPE, I'M JUST TRYING TO GET CANDID SHOTS! I TOOK A FEW GOOD ONES OF MARJORY PARR AND MAYOR PEEVES ARGUING.

Speaking of arguing...

JUST SAY IT, LAYNE: YOU DIDN'T WANT MY DAD TO SELL THE PAINTING AT ALL!

ALL I SAID WAS THAT THE PAINTING BELONGS IN A MUSEUM, NOT IN A PRIVATE COLLECTION!

While everyone was distracted, I got an idea.

FOLLOW ME!

EMPLOYE ONLY

IF WE CAN LOOK AT THE SECURITY TAPES, MAYBE WE CAN PROVE MAYOR PEEVES DIDN'T STEAL THE PAINTING.

SOMEONE'S COMING!

MUSEUM COATS FOR LAUNDRY

ANY NEWS ON THE PARR PAINTING?

Phew! Sometimes Alison and I have to hide in strange places to crack a case!

UM COATS LAUNDRY

When the coast was clear, we found the security tapes. Unfortunately, the rotating camera was pointing away from the painting when it was taken.

HERE'S A SHOT TAKEN RIGHT BEFORE THE PAINTING WAS STOLEN.

AN EMPTY ROOM. NO CLUES HERE.

THIS SHOT WAS TAKEN A MINUTE AFTER THE PAINTING WAS STOLEN. SOMEONE EITHER GOT VERY LUCKY OR KNEW HOW THE CAMERAS WORKED.

YOU SAID IT, ALISON. I KNOW WHO TOOK THE PAINTING.

Do you know who made the painting disappear? All the clues are here. Turn the page for the solution.

Solution: The Case of the
Disappearing Painting

Who stole the painting?

Marjory Parr.
She believed the painting rightfully belonged to her family.

Where is the painting now?

In Marjory's right pant leg. She rolled it up to look like a cast.

Clues

* Layne said the fake painting was a "crummy copy." It was so crummy that Marjory included her own initials (MP), rather than her ancestor's initials (EP).

* Max noticed that Marjory kept switching the position of her crutch as the day went on. If her right leg was actually injured, she'd need to use the crutch under her right arm at all times.

* Marjory volunteered part-time at the museum, so she would know how the security cameras worked.

* Victor Price was carrying a frame in the security camera footage, but it wasn't the Emmeline Parr painting. The real painting was cut out of its frame.

* Alison spotted a box cutter behind Marjory in the gift shop.

Conclusion

Security stopped Marjory on her way out of the museum, and she was caught red-handed. Or, more appropriately, red-panted. She confessed and handed *One Moment* over to the authorities. It was put back in a frame and sold to the highest bidder -- an art collector from Whispering Meadows who promptly donated the painting to the museum. It's now going to be displayed in the museum's permanent collection!

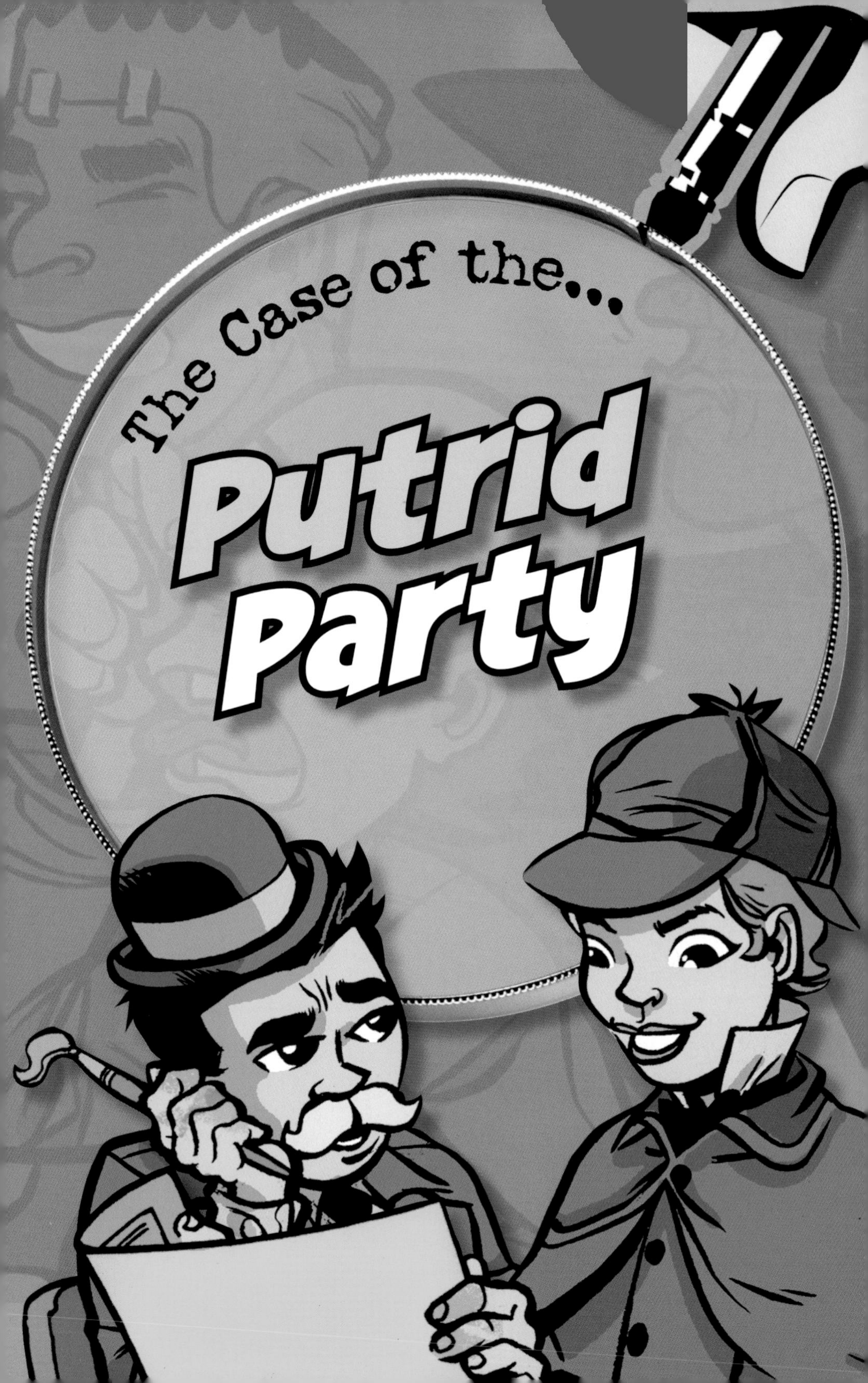
The Case of the...
Putrid
Party

The Case of the Putrid Party

Max Finder, junior high detective, here. My friend Alison and I were helping paint posters during first period for the Halloween dance. It was already a great day, except for one small thing.

I CAN'T BELIEVE I LOST THE COIN FLIP TO BE SHERLOCK HOLMES! I ALWAYS GO AS SHERLOCK.

NOT THIS YEAR, MAX! OR SHOULD I SAY "WATSON"?

HEY! YOU TWO! GOOFING AROUND WON'T GET THE GYM READY FOR THE DANCE. GO HANG UP THOSE POSTERS.

I THINK LESLIE'S LETTING THAT CROWN GO TO HER HEAD!

On the way to the gym, we ran into Zoe "Einstein" Palgrave — our friend and forensic expert — and Jeff "Turtle" Coleman.

COOL COSTUMES, GUYS! WANT TO GO TRICK-OR-TREATING WITH ME LATER?

WE CAN'T, JEFF. THE DANCE IS TONIGHT, REMEMBER?

HOWLI GOOD TIM DANCE

OH, RIGHT. CAN'T WAIT. SEE YOU GUYS THERE!

UH-OH, MAX... LOOK!

WHAM!

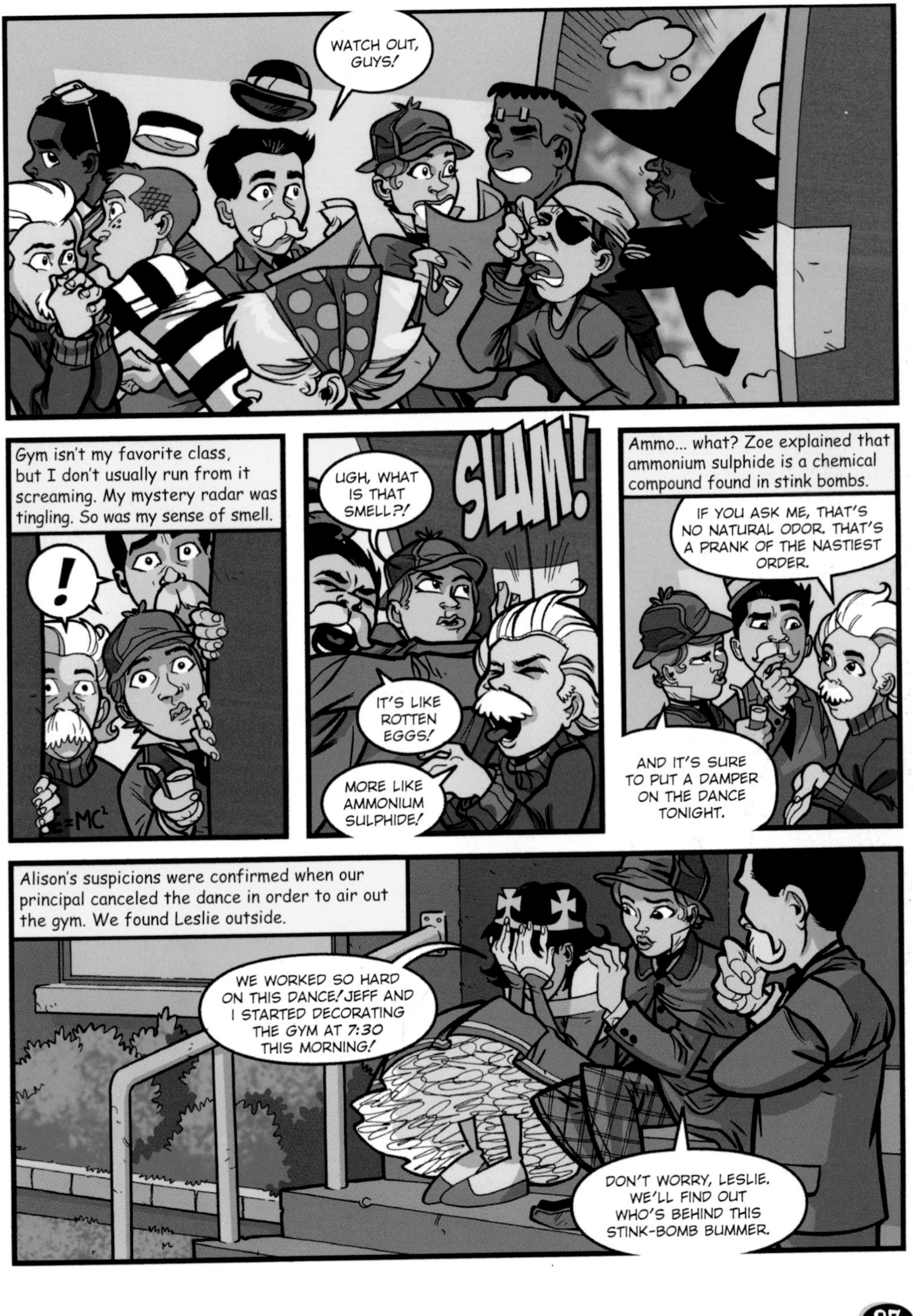
WATCH OUT, GUYS!
Gym isn't my favorite class, but I don't usually run from it screaming. My mystery radar was tingling. So was my sense of smell.
!
E=MC²
SLAM!
UGH, WHAT IS THAT SMELL?!
IT'S LIKE ROTTEN EGGS!
MORE LIKE AMMONIUM SULPHIDE!
Ammo... what? Zoe explained that ammonium sulphide is a chemical compound found in stink bombs.
IF YOU ASK ME, THAT'S NO NATURAL ODOR. THAT'S A PRANK OF THE NASTIEST ORDER.
AND IT'S SURE TO PUT A DAMPER ON THE DANCE TONIGHT.
Alison's suspicions were confirmed when our principal canceled the dance in order to air out the gym. We found Leslie outside.
WE WORKED SO HARD ON THIS DANCE! JEFF AND I STARTED DECORATING THE GYM AT 7:30 THIS MORNING!
DON'T WORRY, LESLIE. WE'LL FIND OUT WHO'S BEHIND THIS STINK-BOMB BUMMER.

Stink bombs? Pranks? Alison and I had an obvious first suspect.

KYLE KRESSMAN! JUST THE PRANKSTER WE'RE LOOKING FOR.

YOU WOULDN'T KNOW ABOUT ANY STINK BOMBS GOING OFF IN THE GYM, WOULD YOU?

OKAY, OKAY. I *DO* HAVE STINK BOMBS. BUT I WOULD NEVER USE THEM AT SCHOOL. I HAVEN'T EVEN OPENED THE PACK. I CAN SHOW YOU.

WHAT?! I DIDN'T OPEN THESE!

Kyle told us that he was in the gym when the smell started, but that he didn't drop the bombs. He'd been looking forward to the dance more than anyone.

DOES ANYONE HAVE ACCESS TO YOUR LOCKER?

EVERYBODY! I KEPT FORGETTING MY LOCKER COMBINATION, SO IT'S ALWAYS UNLOCKED.

WHAT'S THIS PURPLE STUFF?

LOOKS LIKE... POSTER PAINT.

KIND OF LIKE THE PAINT YOU'VE GOT ON YOUR HANDS, MAX? YOU WERE PAINTING POSTERS TODAY, WEREN'T YOU?

JAKE?! YEAH, BUT...

?

NO BUTS, MAX! I'VE GOT MY EYES ON YOU.

Every detective needs a nemesis, and Jake Granger is mine. I was angry he'd accuse me, but Alison seemed even angrier.

WHOOPS! SORRY, JAKE.

BUMP!

WATCH IT, SANTOS!

WHAT'S WITH THE BODYCHECKING ROUTINE, ALISON?

I SAW SOMETHING STUCK TO JAKE'S SHOE AND WANTED TO KNOCK IT OFF WITHOUT HIM NOTICING. GOT YOUR MAGNIFYING GLASS, ZOE?

NICE! IT'S A PIECE OF A STINK BOMB. WHAT'S JAKE DOING WITH THIS STUCK TO HIS SHOE?

HMM. HE DID SEEM PRETTY EAGER TO PIN THE CRIME ON ME.

I HEARD HIM SAY THAT HE WAS MAD BASKETBALL PRACTICE WAS CANCELED FOR THE DANCE.

After school, we gathered outside to go over our case notes.

WELL, SHERLOCK, I'M STUMPED.

IT LOOKS LIKE WE'RE IN THE RIGHT COSTUMES, THEN. I KNOW WHO STUNK UP THE GYM.

SURE YOU GUYS CAN'T COME TRICK-OR-TREATING? MY MOM TOLD ME THIS MORNING SHE'D BE WAITING FOR ME AFTER SCHOOL.

Do you know who sabotaged the dance party? All the clues are here. Turn the page for the solution.

Solution: The Case of the
Putrid Party

Who stink-bombed the gymnasium?

Jeff Coleman.

He wanted to go trick-or-treating, so he took the stink bombs and dropped them in the gym while he was decorating. Jake Granger unknowingly stepped on them in gym class to set them off.

Clues

* The locker next to Kyle's said "Property of Jeff C." That explains how Jeff knew the stink bombs were in Kyle's locker.

* Leslie said Jeff had been at the school since 7:30 a.m. decorating for the dance. That gave Jeff plenty of time to drop the stink bombs off in the gym.

* The package of stink bombs in Kyle's locker had purple paint on it. So did Jeff's hand. Max and Alison had orange paint on their hands.

* Jeff said that his mom was coming to pick him up, and that they'd made the plan that morning. He never intended to go to the dance at all.

* Kyle was telling the truth about wanting to go to the dance. In fact, he was dressed as Disco Stu, a dance-crazy character from *The Simpsons*.

* When Max and Alison saw Jake in the hall, his hands were clean as a whistle. That means he never touched the package of stink bombs in Kyle's locker.

Conclusion

Jeff confessed to the crime and was grounded for a month. The rest of the class went trick-or-treating that night and got dressed up again the next week for a makeup dance. That is, after the gym had aired out.

The Case of
The Game Card Grab

As told by Max Finder

The line outside Game Barn snaked around the corner and halfway up the block. It was a big crowd, but I wasn't surprised. It was a big day. And when I saw John Chu's panicked face at the door of the store, I knew I'd stumbled into a big mystery.

"Max! Get in here." John cracked the front door of the video game store open and ushered me inside. He locked the door behind me, ignoring complaints from a group of teens who must have arrived at midnight to get first spot in line. John was nearly 17 and assistant manager of the Game Barn. He led me to the back of the shop, speaking quickly as he went. "Today's the big draw for the early-access cards for the new Dogtown Malone video game."

"Um, yeah, I know." I held up my backpack plastered with *Dogtown Malone: Zombie World* buttons. One for each time I entered the contest. "I'm here to get my hands on one of the cards."

"You and every other gamer in town," John nodded wearily to the mass of fans with their faces pressed against the glass of the storefront.

Zombie World came out next month and Game Barn was giving away three early-access game cards that let you play the game before anyone else. Gamers who showed up for the draw today got a bonus chance to enter the contest. Judging from the line outside the door, a lot of people wanted to get their hands on those cards. Including me.

"Shouldn't the store be open by now? It's after 10 am." I leaned on the back counter and met the steely gaze of the Dogtown Malone cardboard cutout. It had been standing by the cash register since the contest was announced last month. I had seen that display every time I dropped a ballot into the contest box, but today something was different. There was empty space in his left hand where the game cards should have been.

"That's the problem, Max," John said when he saw I noticed the missing cards. "The cards have been stolen!"

My mystery radar tingled the way it always did when I stumbled on a new case. I grabbed my notebook from my bag and flipped it open.

"We don't have much time," I said. "Tell me what happened."

John took a deep breath, ready to launch into his story, when a round-faced woman stepped out from the manager's office.

"John, I still can't find my keys. You sure you haven't seen them?" She stopped short and rolled her eyes when she saw me. "This is your brilliant detective? A kid with a notebook? We're totally doomed."

I flashed my best "pleased to meet you" smile and reached out to shake her hand. "You must be Deb, the manager. Right?"

"You're a sharp one, kid," Deb said, clearly impressed by my brilliant powers of observation. I decided not to remind her she was wearing a name tag. Even without the tag, though, I would have known her. She's a legend in the Whispering Meadows gaming scene. Her online nickname was "Queen" because she ruled the high score boards of almost every game out there. From the way she glared at John, I could see she ruled her store like a queen, too.

"The draw is at 10:30. You have half an hour to find out who took the cards. If you can't, I'm calling head office and telling them this mess is all your fault."

With that threat hanging in the air, Deb marched to the front of the store.

"Harsh," I said under my breath.

"But true," John slumped his shoulders. "Only Deb and I have keys to the store. I was the last one to see the cards when I locked them in the backroom last night. But Deb doesn't believe me. She thinks I want her job and accused me of taking the cards to make her look bad. "

"She could be doing the same to you." Lukas Hajduk came out from the back wearing a Game Barn vest and carrying a box of old games. "She could have staged the theft to make you look bad to her bosses. They'd never make you manager if they thought you took the cards."

Lukas didn't usually get a high score for his ideas, but what he said made sense. Could Deb be setting up John to take the blame for the theft? Maybe John was the thief and I was the one being set up? I needed more time to work it out.

Deb opened the store and customers streamed in. They all rushed to the Dogtown display. I scrambled out of the way to avoid getting crushed by the mob, all eager to enter the contest one final time.

John pulled me into the backroom, and left Lukas and Deb to deal with the customers. From the doorway, we watched Lukas fumble with a large key ring stamped with the letter Q as he opened the new game console showcase for a customer.

"Lukas did nothing but complain about this job when we closed the store last night. He just told Deb he's quitting today," John whispered. "He's worked here only a month and came in this morning and said he didn't need the money from this job anymore."

"Those cards would sell for a lot of money to a gamer willing to pay," I said.

"No kidding. Crystal Diallo offered all the staff money for the cards. Deb told her to stop bugging us." John checked his watch. "It's strange she isn't here. Every Saturday, she comes into the store and buys something just so she can put another ballot into the contest box."

Deb rushed to the back of the store and hissed at John. "Get out there now! The customers want to see the game cards. It's your mess. You deal with it."

John took a deep breath and marched out of the backroom as Deb began moving large cardboard boxes around. She looked behind each one, sighed, and then moved onto another box. I didn't need detective skills to tell me she still hadn't found her keys. Deb continued her search when I asked her about Crystal.

"She was here earlier. I saw her behind the store talking to Lukas." She stood straight and fixed me with a no-nonsense glare. "This theft is the last thing I need right now. My mom's car broke down yesterday. She won't be happy when I tell her how much it's going to cost to fix it."

Deb's pocket started ringing. She fished out her cellphone, looked at the display screen, and sighed again. "I've gotta take this."

I stuck around and kept my ears tuned to Deb and her phone call.

"I know it's a lot of money," she said into the phone. "But that's how much it's going to cost. If you want it, you're going to have to pay for it."

Things were getting louder in the store, too. Customers pushed against the cash counter like a mass of undead. Their faces twisted in anger, arms waving, and eyes all fixed on one person: John.

"Where are the cards, John?" a customer growled.

"We want them now!" shouted another.

"Gamers!" I stepped out from the doorway with my arms raised. Dozens of game-hungry eyes fell on me. "I know who took the cards. And I know where they are!"

Do you know who stole the game cards? All the clues are here. Turn the page for the solution.

Solution: The Case of the
Game Card Grab

Who stole the game cards?
Lukas Hajduk and
Crystal Diallo.

Clues

* Max became suspicious of Lukas when John said he was quitting his job because he didn't need the money anymore after only working there for a month. The game cards were worth a lot of money and Max suspected that's why Lukas was suddenly quitting.

* John said Lukas helped him close the store the night before. This gave him a chance to take the cards from the backroom.

* Max saw Lukas helping a customer, using a set of keys with a key chain marked with the letter Q. This stood for Deb's gaming handle: "Queen". Lukas had taken her keys the day before to get into the locked backroom.

* Max didn't see the final clue in the mystery -- and that was the problem. Super-fan Crystal Diallo should have been at the store fighting for her chance to win the cards, but she wasn't. That's because she already had the game cards. She showed up early, met Lukas behind the store, and bought the cards from him. That's when Deb saw them.

Conclusion

When confronted with the evidence, Lukas confessed to taking the game cards. He lost his job and agreed to give Crystal her money back. Crystal returned the game cards. Her name was taken from the ballot box and she could only watch as three other lucky gamers -- including Max -- each got a card. Max was happy to crack the case and even happier to crank up his game system and happily hunt some zombies.

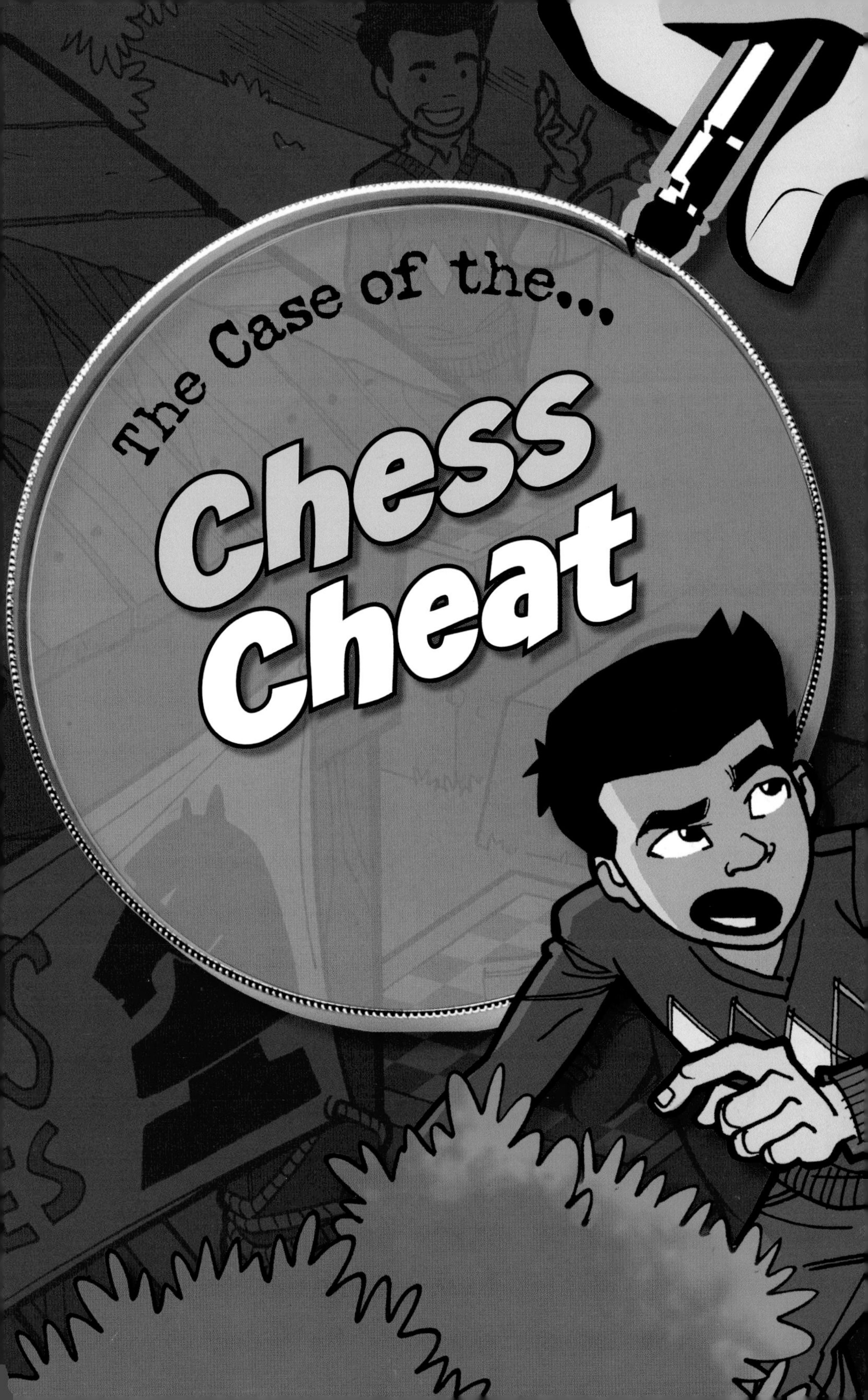
The Case of the...
Chess
Cheat

The Case of the Chess Cheat

Max Finder, junior high detective, here. Whispering Pits Park is always packed. This year, it was also home to the annual class chess tournament. Alison, Zoe, and I were there, but not to check out the chess.

BRR! THIS WEATHER GIVES NEW MEANING TO THE PHRASE "ICING AN OPPONENT," HUH?

VERY FUNNY, MAX. WE'VE GOT A MYSTERY TO SOLVE, SO PUT ON YOUR GAME FACE.

Tournament organizer Dorothy Pafko told us that not everything was going as planned.

I FOUND THIS BY THE CHESS TABLES AT THE END OF THE LAST ROUND.

UM, WHAT IS IT?

YOU MIGHT BE A GREAT DETECTIVE, MAX, BUT YOU SURE DON'T KNOW YOUR SPY GEAR. IT'S A WIRELESS EARPIECE.

I THINK SOMEONE USED IT TO CHEAT. IF THAT'S TRUE, THEN SOME OF THE PLAYERS HAVE BEEN UNFAIRLY OUSTED.

DON'T WORRY, DOROTHY. WE'RE ON THE CASE.

Dorothy postponed the next round for one hour. We huddled together to figure out who, if anyone, was cheating.

I DON'T GET IT. HOW WOULD AN EARPIECE HELP SOMEONE CHEAT?

THE CHEATER COULD USE IT TO RECEIVE INSTRUCTIONS DURING THE MATCH.

BUT WHY WOULD SOMEONE GO TO ALL THAT TROUBLE?

DOROTHY ORGANIZED SOME GREAT PRIZES. THE WINNER GETS AN MP3 PLAYER.

Forensic expert Zoe took off to analyze the earpiece, while Alison and I checked out the tournament bracket in the gazebo.

LEO DUCHARME				ALEX RODRIGUEZ
SAMIR GILL	Samir Gill		Alex Rodriguez	CRYSTAL DIALLO
				ETHAN WEBER
COURTNEY LEGUIN	Nanda Kanwar		Ben McGintley	
NANDA KANWAR		WINNER		

IF SOMEONE'S CHEATING, HE OR SHE IS PROBABLY STILL IN THE GAME.

BASHER! WAIT YOUR TURN!

LET'S SEE. REMAINING PLAYERS ARE ALEX RODRIGUEZ, NANDA KANWAR, SAMIR GILL, AND —

WHAT'S BASHER DOING HERE?

TAKE ANOTHER LOOK AT THE BRACKET, MAX. HE'S IN THE TOURNAMENT.

Quickest case solution ever? Big bully Ben "Basher" McGintley leapt to the top of our suspect list. We tried to catch up with him, but he'd disappeared.

BASHER ALWAYS DISAPPEARS BETWEEN MATCHES. HE'S BEEN SNEAKING AROUND LIKE SOME SORT OF SPY.

ON THE OTHER HAND, ALEX AND SAMIR HAVE BEEN TALKING TRASH NON-STOP.

Alex is our grade's reigning chess champ. Before Samir arrived this year, he also had an unrivaled ego.

SO YOU AND SAMIR SEEM...

HE'S NO MATCH FOR ME ANYWAY. I'VE GOT A SECRET WEAPON UP MY SLEEVE!

YEAH, YOU'D BETTER RUN, ALEX! WHEN I GET THROUGH WITH YOU, YOU'LL BE CHAMP OF THE CONSOLATION ROUND.

SAMIR! THAT LIGHTWEIGHT DOESN'T KNOW A ROOK FROM A PAWN. I'M SURPRISED HE BEAT ANYONE.

We caught up to Samir by the park's lacrosse box.

ALEX MIGHT'VE BEEN THE BEST LAST YEAR, BUT THAT WAS B.M. — BEFORE ME! I COME FROM A FAMILY OF CHESS CHAMPS.

DID ANY OF THEM COME OUT TO CHEER YOU ON?

NO WAY. I WOULDN'T LET 'EM! BESIDES, THEY'RE ALL AT MY SISTER'S DANCE RECITAL.

IT'S TRUE ABOUT THE FAMILY OF CHESS CHAMPS. HIS SISTER, MAYA, IS ONE OF THE BEST PLAYERS IN GRADE 8.

WHOA!

I GOT IT! IT ROLLED INTO THIS BUSH.

HEY!

Turned out the voice from the bush belonged to Alex's little sister, Katlyn.

ENJOYING THE TOURNAMENT, KATLYN?

YES. I MEAN, NO! DON'T TELL ALEX I WAS HERE, OKAY? HE HATES IT WHEN I TAG ALONG WITH HIM. I GOTTA GO!

DID YOU NOTICE THE CHESS MANUAL SHE WAS HOLDING?

HER CELL PHONE COULD BE USED TO TALK TO AN EARPIECE.

THANKS FOR THE ASSIST!

PASS IT, MAYA!

M. GILL

We headed back to the tournament and finally caught a glimpse of Basher — and his goon buddies.

HEY, BASHER! WHEN DID YOU BECOME A CHESS CHUMP?

CAN IT, SHAYNE.

The hour was almost up, but Zoe showed up with some interesting CSI work in the nick of time.

I DUSTED THE EARPIECE FOR FINGERPRINTS AND MADE A DIGITAL IMAGE OF THE FINDINGS. SEE FOR YOURSELF.

I DON'T SEE ANYTHING.

EXACTLY!

SO YOU'RE SAYING THE EARPIECE HASN'T BEEN TOUCHED?

OR... IT HASN'T BEEN TOUCHED BY BARE HANDS.

OKAY, GUYS. I GUESS WE'RE READY TO GET STARTED...

STOP THE CHESSES!

WE KNOW WHO IS CHEATING HIS WAY TO CHECKMATES!

Do you know who the chess cheater is? All the clues are here. Turn the page for the solution.

Solution: The Case of the
Chess Cheat

Who cheated at the chess tournament?

Samir Gill.

He did it with the help of his sister, Maya, who was in the park after all.

Clues

* When Max and Alison stood next to the lacrosse box, they noticed that one of the lacrosse bags was labeled "M. Gill" and had a walkie-talkie sticking out of it. That meant Maya was in the park, and that Samir was lying about his family being at his sister's dance recital.

* Samir was wearing gloves, which would conceal his fingerprints. Alex wore no gloves, and therefore would have left prints on anything he touched.

* Alex's "secret weapon" was actually a four-leaf clover. Max noticed him carrying it around throughout the day.

* Katlyn was carrying a chess manual because she idolizes her brother and wanted to learn more about the game. Because she would be at the park without supervision, her mom asked her to take a cell phone just in case.

* Basher was sneaking around all day because he didn't want to be seen by his buddies, Dwayne and Shayne. He loves chess, but he knew they'd make fun of him for it.

Conclusion

Samir confessed to using the earpiece to cheat. He wanted to impress people in order to make friends, and he told his sister he'd give her the MP3 player if she'd help him win. He was disqualified from the tournament, and Leo Ducharme took his place. Alex and Basher wound up meeting in the finals, and Alex won for the second year in a row -- fair and square.

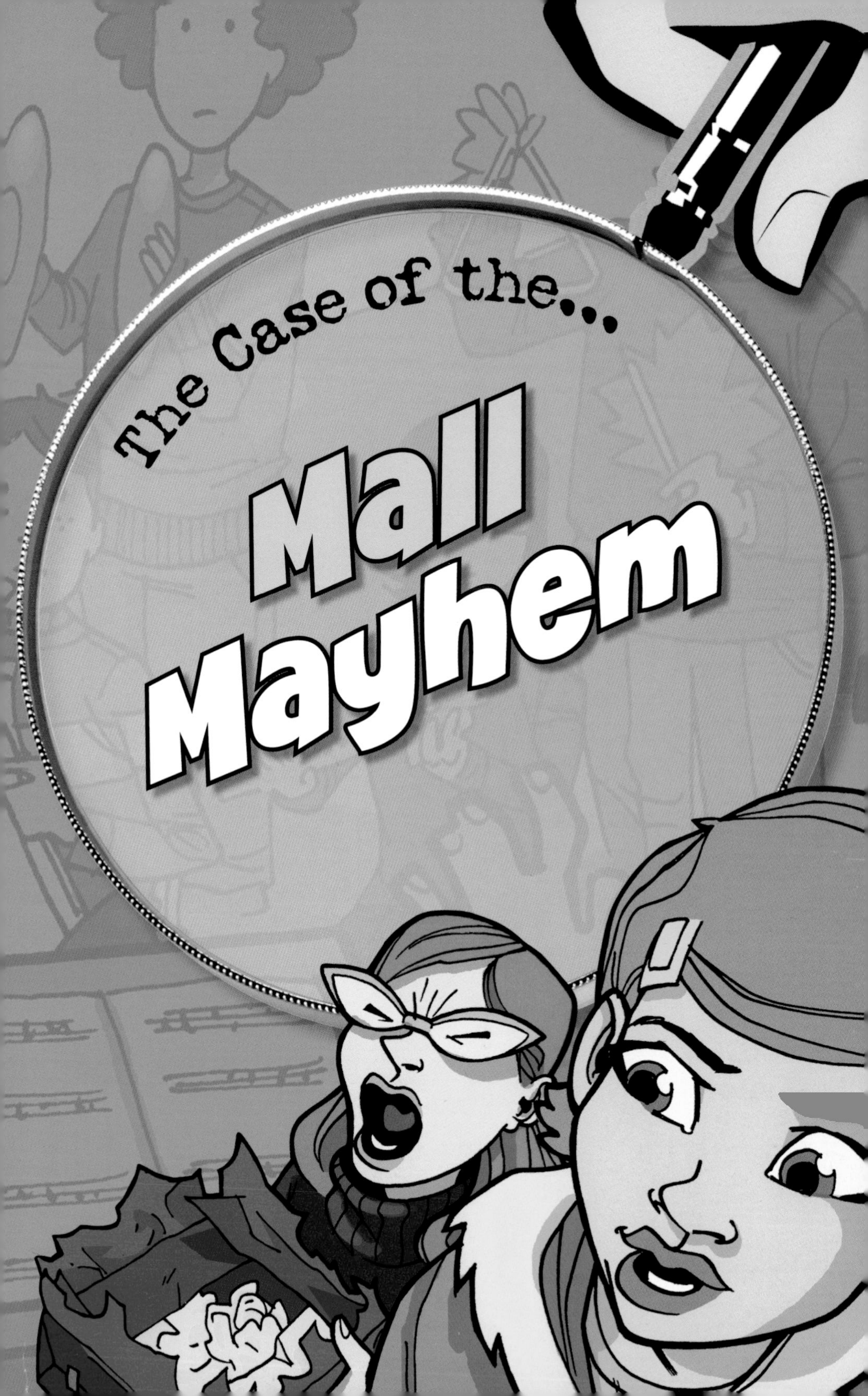
The Case of the...
Mall Mayhem

The Case of the Mall Mayhem

Max Finder here, junior high detective and ho-hum holiday shopper. Alison dragged me to the mall on a Sunday to help her pick out a gift. Luckily, we were almost done.

MISSION ACCOMPLISHED, RIGHT? CAN WE GO NOW?

JUST ONE MORE STOP, MAX. WE HAVE TO GET THIS WRAPPED.

Every year, members of our school's concert band wrap gifts to raise funds for a spring trip. This year, they were about to wrap us up in a mystery.

HOLIDAY GIFT WRAPPING
PROCEEDS GO TO THE CENTRAL MEADOWS JUNIOR HIGH BAND

I'M SORRY, SASHA. I DON'T KNOW WHERE YOUR GIFTS ARE.

PERFORMANCE at the FOUNTAIN SUNDAY at 3:00

Sasha Price is a classmate of ours. We pried her away from Mr. Vostall, the band teacher, and asked her what was going on.

ONE OF THOSE GIFT WRAPPERS STOLE MY GIFTS!

WE CAUGHT THAT PART. FILL US IN ON THE REST.

THEN WE NEED TO FIND THEM! SOMEONE HAS TO PAY FOR THIS!

I brought a CD, a hockey jersey, and some toys to be wrapped yesterday.

Z-BOX2

My chauffeur picked up the gifts when they were done. I didn't notice they were light as a feather until I got home.

JEEVES! THERE'S NOTHING IN HERE!

WHY WOULD ANYONE IN THE SCHOOL BAND WANT TO STEAL YOUR GIFTS?

THEY'RE JUST JEALOUS I'M FIRST CHAIR CLARINET! OR MAYBE THEY'RE MAD THAT I SKIPPED OUT ON WRAPPING GIFTS WITH THEM.

UH... WHAT?

Sasha told us she had lied to get Mr. Vostall to excuse her from gift wrapping. We told her to go cool off, and went to talk to the band teacher.

I CAN'T BELIEVE THIS HAPPENED ON MY WATCH! I REMEMBER SASHA BRINGING IN THE GIFTS. I DROPPED THEM OFF ON LEO DUCHARME'S TABLE.

WE SHOULD ASK LEO IF HE SAW ANYTHING STRANGE YESTERDAY.

DO YOU KNOW HOW WE CAN GET A HOLD OF HIM?

We hung out inside the booth until the shift changed. Stuart DeSilva and Courtney LeGuin were the first to arrive. But Stuart wasn't happy to see us.

HERE'S THE SIGN-IN SHEET. LEO'S SHIFT WILL BE BACK AT 2:00.

SHIFT #3
Stuart DeSilva
Leo DuCharme
COURTNEY LeGUIN
KATE YOON

WHAT ARE YOU TWO DOING BACK HERE? DON'T YOU KNOW THERE'S BEEN A THEFT? THE NEWS IS ALL OVER THE MALL.

COOL IT, STUART! IT'S MAX AND ALISON. WE CAN TRUST THEM.

Courtney took us to her station. She told us she felt really bad for Sasha.

DO YOU KNOW WHO WRAPPED THIS GIFT?

I DON'T WANT TO GET ANYONE IN TROUBLE, BUT THAT DEFINITELY LOOKS LIKE LEO'S HANDIWORK TO ME.

Strike two for Leo? He showed up at the booth a few minutes later. He didn't recognize the box, but he did recognize the packaging.

I WAS USING THIS PAPER DURING MY SHIFT YESTERDAY. BUT I DIDN'T SEE ANY OF SASHA'S GIFTS, I SWEAR!

WAS ANYONE ELSE USING YOUR WRAPPING PAPER?

I DON'T KNOW. IT WAS CRAZY HERE AFTER SASHA CAME. YOU SHOULD'VE HEARD THE STUFF ALL THE GIRLS WERE SAYING ABOUT HER. ESPECIALLY KATE YOON.

HEY, STUART! HELP ME CARRY THE INSTRUMENTS OVER TO THE FOUNTAIN.

MAYBE WE SHOULD TALK TO KATE, HUH, MAX?

HEY! THERE SHE GOES!

So much for the big chase. We caught up with Kate at the stationery store. She didn't deny bad-mouthing Sasha the day before.

SHE BAILED ON US! AND WE'RE NOT ONLY RAISING MONEY FOR THE BAND. WE'RE COLLECTING TOYS FOR CHARITY, TOO. SASHA ONLY CARES ABOUT HERSELF.

SOUNDS LIKE YOU WANT TO GET BACK AT SASHA.

TOTALLY. BUT I DON'T HAVE TIME! IF WE DON'T WRAP FAST ENOUGH, COURTNEY TAKES THE GIFTS RIGHT OFF OUR PILES.

STAPLERS
ll Your Stationery Needs

STAPLE
All Your Sta

I DON'T THINK KATE'S TELLING US EVERYTHING.

LET'S GO BACK AND SCOUR THE BOOTH FOR...

ATTENTION, SHOPPERS. COULD MAX FINDER PLEASE COME TO THE INFORMATION DESK? MAX FINDER?

MAX FINDER? A GIRL LEFT THIS FOR YOU.

IS IT A LOVE NOTE, MAX?

NOT EXACTLY, ALISON.

BUT LOOK! IT'S WRITTEN ON LEO'S WRAPPING PAPER.

BUZZ OFF FINDER!

By the time we got back to the booth, it was closed up for the 3:00 concert. Alison and I decided to check it out.

I CAN'T BELIEVE IT. SASHA SHOWED UP!

MR. VOSTALL! LEO'S MAKING WEIRD NOISES!

IT'S NOT ME! IT'S MY TUBA. THERE'S SOMETHING WRONG WITH IT.

CAN YOU EXPLAIN THIS, MR. DUCHARME?

I THINK I CAN, MR. VOSTALL.

WE KNOW WHO STOLE SASHA'S GIFTS.

Do you know who stole Sasha's gifts? All the clues are here. Turn the page for the solution.

Solution: The Case of the
Mall Mayhem

Who stole Sasha's gifts?

Courtney LeGuin.
She was angry at Sasha for bailing on her bandmates, and stole the gifts to get back at her.

Clues

* Kate said Courtney was such a fast wrapper that she was taking gifts from other people's tables. That explains why Leo never saw the gifts Mr. Vostall dropped off on his table.
* The empty gift box Sasha brought back to the mall was wrapped in Leo's paper, but the crumpled paper inside the box matched Courtney's paper.
* Leo said "the girls" were saying mean things about Sasha, but Courtney told Max and Alison she felt really bad for Sasha. She was lying to make herself look innocent.
* Courtney had access to Leo's tuba when she and Stuart carried it to the concert at the fountain. That's when she planted the jersey in order to frame him.
* The handwriting on the note matched Courtney's from the sign-in sheet.
* The woman at the info desk said "a girl" dropped off the note. Since Max and Alison had just finished talking to Kate at the time the announcement went over the loudspeaker, they deduced that she couldn't have been the note writer.

Conclusion

Courtney confessed to stealing Sasha's gifts and trying to lay the blame on Leo. She apologized to both and returned the stolen stuff. Sasha realized just how angry she'd made everyone, and made it up to them by donating the returned gifts to charity.

The Case of
The Haunted Babysitter

As told by Zoe Palgrave

The heavy oak door swung open before the bell stopped chiming.

"Zoe!" Natasha poked her head through the doorway. She grabbed my shoulder and pulled me into the house. "You made it."

Natasha and I had lived on the same street since I could ride a tricycle. She had her thirteenth birthday last week and started her babysitting career the next day. After taking courses at school and handing out fliers for a week, this was her first job.

"I came as fast as I could," I said. "You said it was an emergency."

"It is," she said, scanning the front yard. "No Max or Alison?"

"Sorry. Just me," I answered. "Max is at a movie and Alison went out to dinner with her family."

Natasha bit her lip as she closed the front door. "Um, okay, I guess."

When your best friends are the school's number-one detectives, you get used to being overlooked. But I didn't mind. I was excited to put my CSI skills to work on my own case for once.

"What's the big mystery? You sounded scared on the phone."

"I am," Natasha squeaked. She jerked her head toward two little kids in animal-print pajamas sitting in the living room. "And so are they."

Two pairs of wide eyes stared back at me. Ruby and Ryan Jigme, twin brother and sister, six years old and terrified judging by the tight hugs they were giving the stuffed animals in their laps.

"I've got to get them in bed and off to dreamland before their parents return or this job could be my last," Natasha said.

"So you need me to help put them to bed?" This wasn't exactly working out to be the case I'd hoped for.

"No, no. Under normal circumstances I could totally do it." Natasha shot a quick glance at the two kids. "But since we saw the ghost, they probably won't go to sleep until they graduate high school."

"Did you say 'ghost'?" I tried not to smile. "You know there's no such thing as ghosts, right?"

"Tell that to them," Natasha nodded to the twins.

Some detectives use their intuition to solve mysteries. I use science. As a scientist, I know that every ghost story has a logical explanation: wires, smoke, mirrors, whatever. But I had a feeling getting two scared first graders to believe that would be anything but simple.

"Follow me." Natasha led us through the house to the kitchen. Ruby and Ryan trailed behind us. Natasha pointed through the window overlooking the backyard. "We were sitting here having cookies and milk. Then a white flapping ghost flew straight toward the window."

"It screeched like a monster!" Ruby said. "It was spooky."

"'Spooky'? More like 'silly'!"

Ruby and Ryan's 10-year-old brother stood at the top of the stairs leading to the basement.

"How would you know, Kaden?" Ryan glared at his older brother.

"Yeah, you weren't even here when we saw the ghost!" Ruby scowled.

"Where have you been?" Natasha checked her watch. "I've been looking for you."

"I was in the basement watching TV," Kaden smirked. "In case you forgot, I'm ten years old. I can probably babysit better than anyone in this room! I definitely wouldn't be scaring little kids with stories of ghosts in the backyard."

Kaden stomped back down to the basement. Within seconds the sound of the TV came blaring up to the top of the stairs.

"He's just mad because his parents say he has to go to bed at the same time as the twins," Natasha shrugged. "Normally, he's a nice kid."

I zipped up my coat. I really wanted to see the backyard and Natasha's "ghost."

Natasha sent the twins to hang out with Kaden and took me through the mud room to the back door. We picked our way around several piles of laundry — some clean, some wet and waiting for the drier — and I squatted down beside a row of boots beside the door. The largest pair of kids' boots was still covered in chunks of melting snow.

"When were you all outside?" I asked.

"Three hours ago. We came in for dinner, baths, snack, and bed."

"Plenty of melting time," I said and stepped out the back door.

The swhooshing sound of ice skates came from the backyard next door. A puck slammed into the wooden fence, shaking it on impact.

"Goal!" a voice shouted. A scarf-covered head peered over. "Hey sis! How's babysitting going? Need me to check the closet for monsters?"

The boy disappeared to a chorus of laughs from his side of the fence.

"Julian," Natasha said shaking her head. "My brother. He made an ice rink last week. He's been on it all night with his friends."

"Maybe they thought it'd be fun to scare little sister on her first babysitting job," I said, noticing a set of footprints leading from the fence to the center of the yard.

"That'd totally be Julian," she said quickly. "He's jealous that I'll be making more money than him with my babysitting jobs."

I walked through the snow to the far end of the yard, where three tall pine trees stood in a row. Natasha came up beside me and stopped when she saw me staring at the snow.

"We didn't come back here before." Natasha pointed beyond the tall pines to the next yard. "That's Leslie Chang's house."

"Don't the Jigmes usually hire Leslie to babysit?" I asked.

"Yes, but they're trying me out because I offered a lower rate, " Natasha said. "I waved at Leslie earlier, but she just scowled at me."

The lights from the Chang house lit up a second set of footprints in the yard. These ones led from the Jigme's house to the largest pine tree.

A rusty pulley hung from the tree. A thin blue plastic laundry line ran through the pulley straight to the Jigme's house. I clipped a mitten to a clothes peg and tugged the line. The cold metal pully screeched loudly as the line ran through it. My mitten zoomed toward the house.

"That sounds like the ghost!" Natasha gasped.

"Exactly." I reeled my mitten back. Another ghost story revealed to be wires and tricks. "The haunter launched the ghost from here. Then made their getaway."

Natasha climbed the smooth snow bank piled up along the fence backing onto Leslie's house. She was high up enough to almost step over the fence. "With this pile of snow, Leslie could easily have made a quick getaway."

The hockey players cheered another goal from Natasha's backyard.

"My brother could be the haunter, too." Natasha threw her arms up in frustration. "This was a waste of time. The Jigmes will be home soon, the haunter is long gone, and the twins are still too scared to sleep."

"Relax, Natasha. I know who's haunting your babysitting job."

Do you know? All the clues are here. Turn the page for the solution.

Solution: The Case of the
Haunted Babysitter

Who is haunting Natasha and the kids?

Kaden Jigme.

Clues

* Zoe knew Kaden had a motive when he complained about being too old for a babysitter.

* The snow-covered boots in the mud room belonged to Kaden and proved he had been outside and not in the basement watching TV.

* Zoe knew that footprints are like snapshots. She noticed the prints leading from the back door of the Jigme's house led directly to the pulley and the start of the laundry line. That's the path Kaden took to complete his crime.

* The footprints leading from Julian's backyard, meanwhile, merely led to the middle of the yard. That means he never approached the pulley at all.

* Finally, the snowbank leading to Leslie's house was totally smooth. That means no one had walked on it at all.

Conclusion

When confronted with the evidence, Kaden admitted to trying to make Natasha look like a bad babysitter by scaring his brother and sister so they wouldn't go to bed. He told them how he took a wet sheet from the mud room and attached it to the pulley, sending it whizzing towards the kids as they ate cookies and milk in the kitchen.

Natasha put the twins to bed, and they were fast asleep by the time Mr. and Mrs. Jigme arrived home. When Kaden's parents heard about his prank, they grounded him and made him do the family laundry for a week. The Jigmes were so impressed with Natasha, they made her their regular babysitter. Zoe often comes over to read the twins bedtime stories and check the backyard for ghosts.

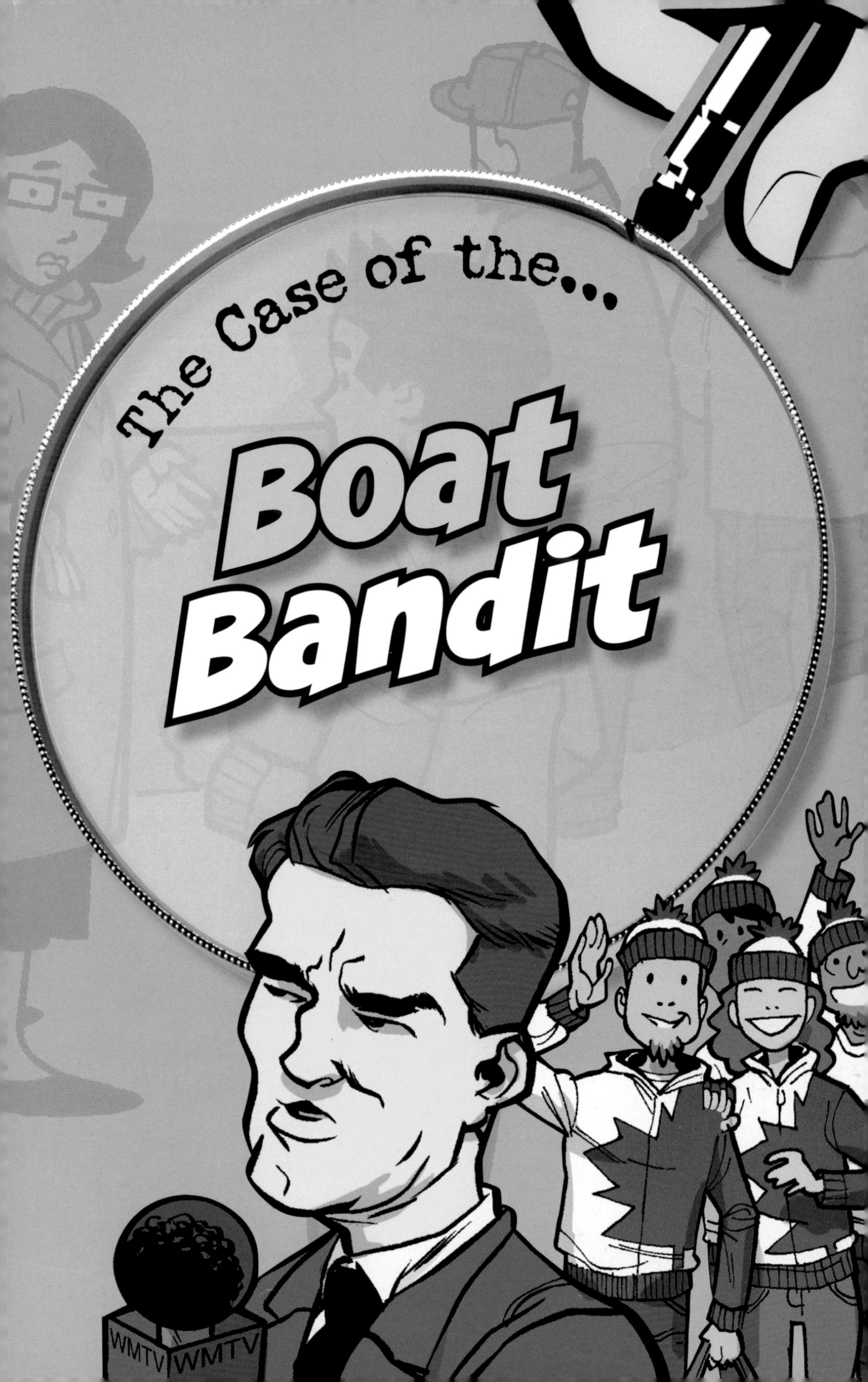
The Case of the...
Boat Bandit
WMTV
WMTV

The Case of the Boat Bandit

Max Finder here, junior high detective and bag-toting tourist. My TV-producer mom was on assignment covering the Vancouver Olympics, and I luckily got to tag along — if I agreed to help carry stuff.

THIS IS SO EXCITING, MOM! NEXT OLYMPICS, I'LL BE READY FOR THE PACK MULE EVENT.

SHH! MILES IS STARTING TO FILM BULL.

OKAY, MILES. ON ME IN FIVE, FOUR, THREE...

AHOY! BULL O'WILEY HERE FOR WHISPERING MEADOWS TV. I'M ABOARD A B.C. FERRY ON A DAY TRIP WITH CANADA'S OLYMPIANS.

OKAY, THAT'S GOOD FOR AN OPENER. NOW...

Ouch! Shelby Sharpie is a slick snowboarder — but today she was tumbling like a gymnast.

YOU'LL PAY FOR MY DRY CLEANING!

HA! THAT TUMBLE WAS GREAT. I CAUGHT IT ALL ON TAPE!

MILES! LEAVE THE POOR GIRL ALONE.

As Bull and Miles walked off, we were left to clean up the gear.

SORRY ABOUT THAT, MAX. LET'S GET THESE TAPES PUT AWAY.

HEY EVERYBODY! WHALES OFF THE PORT BOW!

We ran outside but we didn't catch a glimpse of the whales.

SHOOT, I GUESS WE MISSED THEM.

BUMMER, DUDE! A WOMAN IN A RED JACKET TOLD ME THE WATER WAS TEEMING WITH BELUGAS.

UM, DID WE LEAVE THE BAGS OPEN LIKE THAT?

OUR TAPES! THEY'RE MISSING.

BUT ALL THE CAMERA EQUIPMENT IS STILL HERE. MAYBE SOMEONE WANTED THAT FOOTAGE OF SHELBY FALLING.

IF IT ISN'T THE CREW FROM WHIMPERING MEADOWS. TURNS OUT YOU'RE NOT THE ONLY ONES WITH A SIDNEY CROSBY INTERVIEW!

That's Chaz Wheatley from Sunn TV. Bull must've been bragging earlier about his exclusive sit-down with the Canadian hockey hero.

My mom stayed with our gear, while I searched for eyewitnesses. The kids in the play area behind us said they saw someone go into our bags, but they had trouble agreeing on the details.

I SAW HIM. HE WAS TALL!

NO WAY! HE WAS SMALL.

HE WAS LIKE YOU!

ME?! WHY ME?

HE HAD A BADGE!

MEDIA
Max Finder

I needed to run through some thoughts, so I called up Alison and filled her in on the situation.

THE TAPE MAKES BOTH SHELBY AND BULL LOOK BAD. EITHER ONE OF THEM COULD HAVE WANTED THAT TAPE LOST.

I JUST DID AN INTERNET SEARCH ON MILES. TURNS OUT HE HAS A POPULAR GOOTUBE CHANNEL. MAYBE HE PLANS TO TURN THE TRIPPING CLIP INTO A VIRAL VIDEO.

Speaking of Miles...

THANKS, AL. GOTTA GO.

THE VIDEO IS GOLD! I CAN'T WAIT TO POST IT TO MY CHANNEL. IT'S GOING TO TAKE ME TO THE TOP!

THERE YOU ARE!

Miles would have to wait. I was the detective, but Shelby was the one shaking me down.

THAT VIDEO YOUR CREW TOOK COULD RUIN ME! I'D BE THE JOKE OF THE HALF-PIPE. IF IT SHOWS UP ON THE INTERNET, MAX, YOUR MOM'S IN BIG TROUBLE.

SHE DOESN'T WANT TO PUT IT ON THE 'NET!

MAYBE YOUR MOM DOESN'T, BUT I DON'T TRUST HER CAMERA GUY. I'D KEEP AN EYE ON HIM.

NO PROBLEM, SHELBY. I'VE GOT MY EYES ON HIM RIGHT NOW.

I followed Miles to the observation deck, where he met up with Chaz Wheatley.

HERE'S THE TAPE I TOLD YOU ABOUT EARLIER. JUST MAKE SURE TO GIVE CREDIT TO SUNN TV.

THANKS. I CAN'T WAIT TO POST IT!

I moved in for a closer look...

CRASH

...but I gave away my position.

HEY, KID!

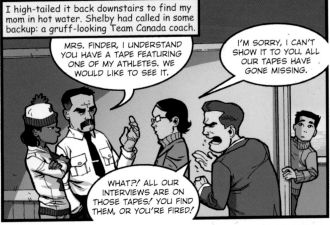

I high-tailed it back downstairs to find my mom in hot water. Shelby had called in some backup: a gruff-looking Team Canada coach.

MRS. FINDER, I UNDERSTAND YOU HAVE A TAPE FEATURING ONE OF MY ATHLETES. WE WOULD LIKE TO SEE IT.

I'M SORRY, I CAN'T SHOW IT TO YOU. ALL OUR TAPES HAVE GONE MISSING.

WHAT?! ALL OUR INTERVIEWS ARE ON THOSE TAPES! YOU FIND THEM, OR YOU'RE FIRED!

NOT SO FAST, MR. O'WILEY! I KNOW WHO FILCHED OUR FOOTAGE.

Do you know who stole the tapes? All the clues are here. Turn the page for the solution.

Solution: The Case of the
Boat Bandit

Who stole the tapes?

Chaz Wheatley.

But he didn't want the footage of Shelby tripping into Bull. He wanted to steal the interview Bull did with Sidney Crosby.

Clues

* A woman in a red jacket said the ocean was "teeming with belugas." Max knew this wasn't true -- belugas don't swim in those waters. When he saw Chaz hanging around with a woman in a red jacket, he knew that Chaz used her to distract Max and his mom.

* After the theft, Max noticed a gold button in the bag of video equipment. Later on, he also noticed that Chaz was missing a button from the right cuff of his jacket. Chaz lost the button when stealing the tapes.

* The kids said the thief was wearing a media badge, and they all said "he." That means it couldn't have been Shelby or the woman in the red jacket.

* Chaz gave Miles a tape for his GooTube channel, but it wasn't the footage of Shelby falling. Max noticed the tape had a picture of a sun on it -- that meant it was property of Chaz's station, Sunn TV, and not Whispering Meadows TV.

* Bull was shocked and disappointed that the interviews had been lost. Stealing the blooper video would mean losing all his hard work, and he'd never do that.

Conclusion

When Max presented his evidence, Chaz confessed to stealing the tapes. He gave the tapes back (they were stuffed in his pockets), and had his media accreditation revoked for the rest of the Olympics. Max's mom erased the tripping clip, and Shelby went home happy.

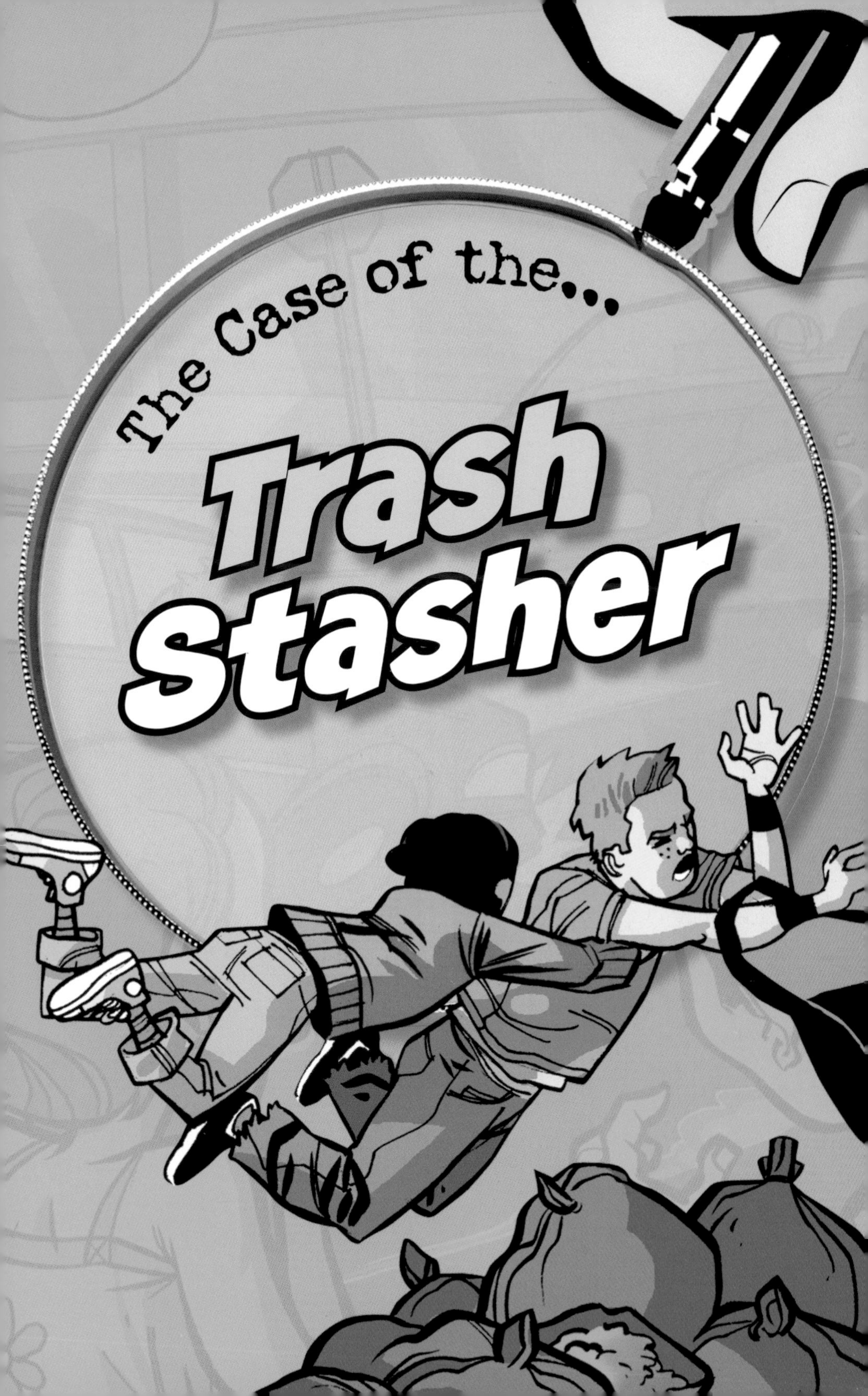
The Case of the...
Trash Stasher

The Case of the
Trash Stasher

Max Finder, junior high detective, here. It was spring break in Whispering Meadows. A garbage strike had everyone in town on edge, but my best friend Alison was still happy to see me.

WELCOME BACK, MAX!

COOL IT, ALISON. I WAS JUST GONE FOR THE WEEKEND.

WHAT'S GOING ON HERE?

AS YOUR MAYOR, I REGRET TO INFORM YOU THAT SANITATION WORKERS ARE STILL ON STRIKE. IF YOU CAN HAVE JUST A LITTLE MORE PATIENCE...

"PATIENCE"?!

THAT'S WHAT YOU SAID LAST WEEK!

The lady in the glasses is my neighbor Mrs. Briggs. The other is Ms. Eisner, Whispering Meadows' best lawyer.

MY SON, ZACK, HAS MADE THREE TRIPS THERE THIS WEEK! IT TAKES TWO HOURS EACH TIME.

I'M NOT MAKING ONE MORE TRIP OUT TO THAT DUMP!

YOU'VE GOT TO END THE STRIKE, MAYOR PEEVES, OR ELSE I'M GOING TO MAKE A BIG STINK OVER THIS.

WOW. THEY'RE REALLY ANGRY. THINGS HAVE DEFINITELY HIT A BOILING POINT.

THAT'S NOT THE HALF OF IT. YOU SHOULD GET A WHIFF OF MY NEIGHBORHOOD.

On our way to Alison's house we bumped into Zack, Ms. Eisner's son. He goes to Whispering Meadows High School. He told us he'd been driving his family's trash out to the dump.

COME ON, ZACK! LET'S GO.

IT'S A REAL DRAG, BUT AT LEAST I GET TO BORROW MY MOM'S CAR. I CAN HIT THE SKATE PARK ON THE SLY!

ISN'T THE DUMP ON THE OTHER SIDE OF TOWN FROM THE SKATE PARK?

SEE YOU LATER, LITTLE DUDES!

As we got closer to Alison's house, the smell got worse. Something was up.

UGH. SEE WHAT I MEAN, MAX?

THERE'S GOT TO BE AN EXPLANATION FOR THIS. LET'S SPREAD OUT. YOU CHECK ACROSS THE STREET.

MAX! GET OVER HERE.

No wonder the neighborhood stunk! Alison had stumbled onto a mountain of garbage.

GET OUT YOUR NOSEPLUGS, ALISON. SOMEONE'S DUMPING HERE ILLEGALLY, AND I SMELL A MYSTERY.

We hopped the fence for a closer look. The backyard belonged to the old Grierson place. The Griersons were Alison's neighbors, but they'd moved out months ago and the house was empty.

YOU HEARD MRS. BRIGGS EARLIER. SHE TOLD MAYOR PEEVES THAT SHE'D TAKEN HER LAST TRIP OUT THERE. AND ZACK'S MOM DIDN'T SEEM TOO HAPPY EITHER.

WHO WOULD DO SOMETHING LIKE THIS? I MEAN, IT TAKES ONLY 15 MINUTES TO DRIVE TO THE DUMP.

We picked up a couple bags and took them to show Zoe, our friend and forensic expert. She dug right into the trash to look for clues.

FOUND ANYTHING, ZOE?

NOTHING YET. NO BILLS, LETTERS, OR ANYTHING WITH AN ADDRESS. THIS BAG COULD BELONG TO JUST ABOUT ANYONE.

IT'S AN ESSAY. BUT THE INK'S SMUDGED. I CAN'T READ THE NAME.

HOLD ON. WHAT'S THIS?

I'LL USE MY MAGNIFYING GLASS.

BEN McGIN

CALL OFF THE SEARCH. THIS PAPER BELONGS TO... BEN McGINTLEY.

BASHER?!

Basher McGintley is our town's biggest bully. He loves messing with people, so the profile fits him perfectly.

THAT'S GOOD, RIGHT? WE'VE GOT OUR SUSPECT. LET'S GO FIND BASHER.

NOT SO FAST. WE NEED MORE EVIDENCE, AND WE CAN'T LET HIM KNOW WE'RE ON THE CASE.

WHAT HAVE YOU GOT IN MIND, MAX?

We went back to Alison's and hunkered down on the front porch to watch and wait.

HEY. THAT'S BASHER. AND HE'S CARRYING A BIG BAG. LET'S GET HIM!

ZOE! WAIT!

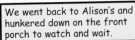

THANKS FOR LETTING ME COME ON THE STAKEOUT, MAX.

NO PROBLEM, ZOE. JUST KEEP LOW AND LOOK OUT FOR —

WHA -- ?!

IT'S... HOCKEY GEAR!

BUT WHAT ABOUT THIS?

IT'S AN "F"! I CHUCKED IT OVER THE FENCE LAST WEEK AFTER I SAW SOME GUY THROW A GARBAGE BAG OVER THERE.

SORRY I RUINED THE STAKEOUT, MAX. NOW WE MAY NEVER KNOW WHO DID IT.

NEVER SAY NEVER, ZOE. I KNOW WHO'S DOING THE DUMPING.

AND I KNOW WHY.

While Zoe and I helped Basher up, Alison noticed someone behind us. In all the commotion we hadn't even seen the car pull up to the curb.

MAX! LOOK!

Do you know who stashed the trash? All the clues are here. Turn the page for the solution.

Solution: The Case of the
Trash Stasher

Who stashed the trash?
Zack Eisner.

He wanted extra time at the skate park, so he started dumping his family's trash at the Grierson place.

Clues
* It takes 15 minutes to get to the dump (and another 15 minutes back), but Ms. Eisner said it took Zack almost two hours to make a single trip. He wasn't going to the dump at all. He was going to the skate park with his friends.
* Max and Alison noticed the car driving away had two working tail lights. Mrs. Briggs's car had one tail light covered with duct tape when they saw her downtown.
* Max noticed a green coffee cup with a white stripe in the trash. He had seen Ms. Eisner drinking from a similar coffee cup earlier in the day. Mrs. Briggs, on the other hand, was drinking from a brown coffee cup.
* Basher wasn't the culprit because he was busy being helped up when the real trash stasher tossed his garbage bag over the fence.
* Basher said he saw "some guy" throw a garbage bag over the fence earlier. This eliminates Mrs. Briggs and Ms. Eisner from the list of suspects.

Conclusion
Ms. Eisner confirmed the trash was theirs and Zack confessed. He apologized to everyone in the neighborhood and cleaned up the backyard of the Grierson place himself. Zack wasn't allowed to borrow his mom's car for a year, but he got a lot of skateboarding in riding to and from community service -- picking up trash!

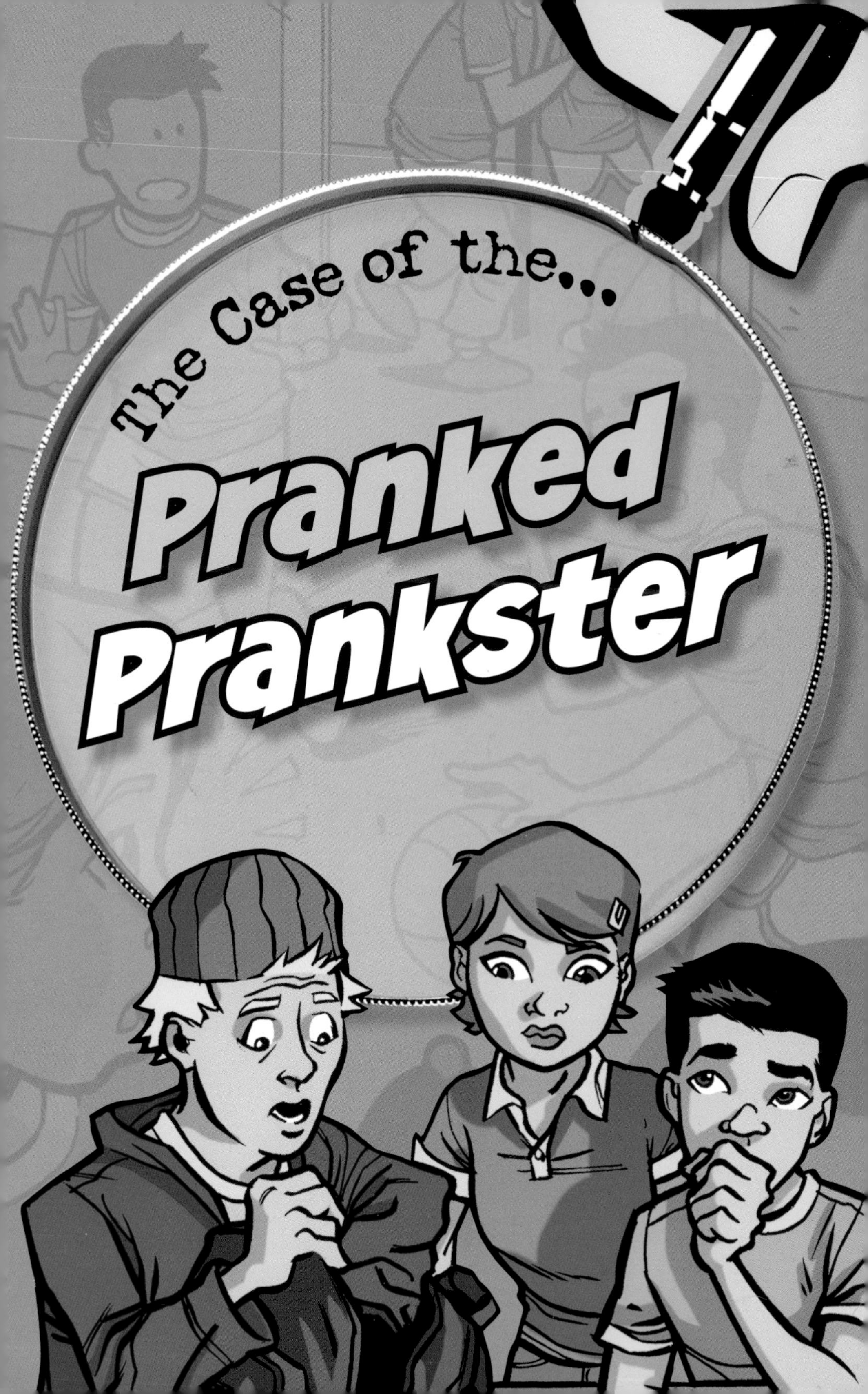
The Case of the...
Pranked
Prankster

The Case of the
Pranked Prankster

Max Finder here, junior high detective and moving target. It had been a week since April Fool's Day, but the pranks kept coming from our class.

MAX! ALISON! SOMEONE STOLE MY BACKPACK!

SMILE, MAX! YOU'RE ON KYLE CAMERA.

Punk'd! Meet Kyle Kressman, prankster extraordinaire. Last week he convinced Josh Spodek and Leslie Chang to study for a geometry test we didn't even have.

KYLE! COME SEE ME, PLEASE.

I CAN'T BELIEVE WE FELL FOR THAT. EVERYONE'S LAUGHING AT US.

I DON'T KNOW. PEOPLE ARE TIRED OF KYLE'S PRANKS. MAYBE THE JOKE'S ON HIM THIS TIME.

After school, we overheard Leslie talking to herself.

SPEAKING OF KYLE...

KYLE JUST DOESN'T KNOW WHEN TO QUIT!

MAX! SOMEONE STOLE MY BACKPACK.

RIGHT... WE'RE GOING TO FALL FOR THAT TWO TIMES IN THE SAME DAY.

SEE YOU LATER, KYLE.

Another day, another prank? Most people were using the morning period to finish up presentations, but Kyle was trying to convince us his bag really was stolen.

I GOT HERE EARLY AND SEARCHED THE SCHOOLYARD. IT'S NOWHERE!

YEAH RIGHT, KYLE! GO WORK ON YOUR PRESENTATION AND LEAVE US ALONE.

THAT'S THE WHOLE POINT. MY PRESENTATION WAS IN MY BAG! I HAD A BASEBALL IN THERE SIGNED BY JOE CARTER.

I'M GOING TO FAIL IF I CAN'T GET IT BACK BY THIS AFTERNOON!

HEY, DID ANYBODY LOSE A...

MY BACKPACK!

Ethan Webster told us he'd found the backpack out by the basketball courts. He and Josh play there most mornings.

THE BALL IS MISSING. NOW DO YOU BELIEVE THAT SOMEONE STOLE IT, MAX?

ALL RIGHT, ALL RIGHT! WHO KNEW YOU HAD THE BALL, AND WHAT WERE YOU DOING WHEN THE BAG WENT MISSING?

We were here in the library. I was working with Ethan, Josh, Nanda, and Leslie. The guys were being secretive about their presentation, so I told everyone about mine.

HERE IT IS!

WHOA!

I passed the ball around, and everyone seemed impressed. That is, *almost* everyone...

JOE CARTER? WHO CARES ABOUT HIM ANYMORE?

ARE YOU KIDDING, JOSH?! CARTER IS A TORONTO BLUE JAYS LEGEND!

AFTER WE FINISHED UP I WENT BACK TO HOMEROOM. I KNOW THE BALL WAS IN MY BAG WHEN I GOT MY CAMERA OUT TO PRANK... WELL, YOU KNOW.

THAT MEANS THE BAG COULDN'T HAVE BEEN STOLEN IN THE LIBRARY.

BUT IT DOESN'T CHANGE OUR LIST OF SUSPECTS. THE THIEF KNEW WHERE TO LOOK.

We started off with Leslie.

PART OF KYLE'S PRESENTATION IS MISSING. DID YOU SEE ANYTHING WHEN YOU GUYS WERE WORKING TOGETHER?

I DIDN'T TOUCH HIS STUPID BASEBALL! I WASN'T EVEN THERE WHEN HE SHOWED IT OFF. I WAS IN THE ART ROOM GETTING SPARKLES FOR MY POSTER. I BET ONE OF THOSE JOCKS ETHAN OR JOSH TOOK IT.

JOSH HAS THE MOTIVE, BUT ETHAN BROUGHT THE BAG RIGHT INTO CLASS. NOT EXACTLY THE SLY MOVEMENTS OF A CRIMINAL.

MAYBE ETHAN DID THAT TO APPEAR INNOCENT. KYLE SAID HE WAS INTERESTED IN THE BALL.

We bumped into Josh — literally — as he ran down the hallway.

OOF!

HEY!

WHY SO RUSHED, JOSH? KNOW ANYTHING ABOUT KYLE'S MISSING BASEBALL?

ME? NO WAY! I DON'T KNOW ANYTHING ABOUT ANY BALLS.

IF YOU WANT A SUSPECT, TALK TO NANDA. SHE TOLD US HER DAD WANTED TO BUY THE BALL, BUT KYLE'S DAD OUTBID HIM FOR IT.

BRRING!

Before we could ask anything else, Josh took off.

JOSH, WAIT UP!

SORRY, MAX! GOTTA GO.

Next on our list of suspects was Nanda. She told Alison that the owner of the sports card shop had promised the ball to her dad, but that Kyle's dad had offered more money at the last minute.

KYLE AND HIS DAD ARE THE REAL CROOKS HERE. I'LL BE GLAD IF SOMEONE TOOK THAT BALL.

DID YOU SEE WHO MIGHT HAVE STOLEN IT?

THE FOUR OF US PASSED IT AROUND AND GAVE IT BACK TO KYLE. HE PROBABLY TOOK IT HIMSELF TO PRANK YOU GUYS AGAIN.

Meanwhile, I noticed something suspicious happening on my side of the gym.

AND THEN YOU GIVE YOUR LINE, AND THEN I'LL PASS YOU THE BALL.

HEY! DO YOU TWO HAVE HALL PASSES?

We spent a few minutes in the principal's office and made it back to class just in time for presentations.

OKAY, KYLE, IF YOU CAN'T GIVE YOUR PRESENTATION, THEN WE'LL MOVE ON TO...

HOLD UP, MR. REED! KYLE'S BALL REALLY WAS STOLEN.

AND WE KNOW WHO TOOK IT.

Do you know who took the baseball? All the clues are here. Turn the page for the solution.

Solution: The Case of the
Pranked Prankster

Who stole Kyle's baseball?
Leslie Chang.
She was mad about Kyle tricking her into studying for the fake geometry test and wanted to get back at him.

How did she do it?
While Kyle was talking to Mr. Reed, Leslie took his backpack. She kept the baseball, and ditched Kyle's stuff by the basketball courts the next day to make it look like Ethan or Josh had stolen the ball.

Clues
* Alison noticed Leslie was wearing a black backpack after school on the day of the theft. The next day, she had a pink pack in the library. The black backpack was Kyle's.
* Max told Leslie that "part of Kyle's presentation" was missing. But Leslie immediately knew it was a baseball.

* Nanda says "the four of us" passed the ball around. That means Leslie was lying about not being in the library.
* When Max and Alison followed Josh and Ethan, they saw that they were practicing their presentation on basketball star Steve Nash. The "ball" they were talking about was a basketball.
* At the start of class, Kyle hadn't produced the ball and was ready to take an "F." That means he didn't take it himself.

Conclusion
Leslie admitted to stealing the ball. Mr. Reed gave her detention, but she perked up the following week when she aced a pop quiz -- on geometry! Kyle promised to keep his pranks to a minimum -- until next April Fool's Day, that is!

The Case of
The Snatched Skateboard

As told by Alison Santos

"Andrea, slow down!" I wheezed, sun-blind and out of breath. "This is my first day running with you, remember?"

Six driveways up the road, Andrea Palgrave circled back and jogged toward me. With the early morning sun rising in the east and at her back, I couldn't see her face but I could see the spring in her step. She wasn't even breathing hard.

"All right Alison, we'll take it easy. You're a bigger whiner than Zoe!"

"At least your sister was smart enough to stay in bed this morning." I slowed to a walk and showed Andrea my watch. As if she needed to see it. "It's seven o'clock in the morning. I can't believe I let you talk me into these before-school runs."

"I run this road every morning at this time. You'll get used to it." Andrea ran on the spot, clearly eager to get moving again. "You're the one who needs to kick butt at this year's cross-country meet. This is the only way to do it."

"I know, I know." I started running again, breaking into my best teacher voice. "Running in the morning is the best way to start your day and avoid the heat of the sun."

"Do I sound that bad?" Andrea was off again, powering her way along the tree-lined street.

"At this time in the morning everything sounds bad!"

Early mornings and I don't get along, but I was running around the block at seven A.M. for two reasons: My Big Mouth and Max Finder. The Whispering Meadows cross-country meet was a month away and

Max was already bragging how he was the fastest detective in town. I don't get along with running either, but that didn't stop me from announcing to Max and the entire cafeteria that I was going to beat him in this year's race.

Now I was up before the birds, struggling to catch Andrea, the cross-country machine. She's won the all-city finals three years in a row. She was also my only hope of saving my reputation and keeping Max quiet once and for all.

My legs felt like sacks of sand as I finally lurched over to the bend in the road where Andrea was waiting. Sun at her back, I still couldn't see her face but I didn't need to. I knew she was smiling and having fun.

"Help me, Andrea!" a voice called from a nearby driveway.

Leo Ducharme stumbled out from behind a wide oak. His face was pale and streaks of red ran down his legs from two skinned knees.

Andrea eased Leo to the grass near the edge of the road. He's small for his age and normally looks younger than his 13 years, but now he looked like a pre-schooler.

"He took it! I tried to stop him, but he was too strong." Leo's eyes went wide when he saw me. "Alison. You're here?"

"Who took what, Leo?" I scanned the street. There was no one around.

Leo slurped from my water bottle and caught his breath. "The skateboard," he said finally.

"Who's skateboard?" Andrea stood, towering over Leo. An edge crept into her voice.

Leo looked up sheepishly. "Your skateboard."

"I knew it!" Andrea growled. "I lend you my skateboard and you get it stolen."

"You were going to sell it anyway, remember." Leo looked hurt and it wasn't just his cut knees. "That's why you let me borrow it."

"I let you test ride it for a few days because you were going to buy it." Andrea glared at Leo. She turned to me, her eyes quickly narrowing and her voice steady as a marathoner's pace. "We've got to get that board back. I was going to use the money from selling it to buy new running shoes for the meet."

I took back my water bottle. "Tell me what happened, Leo."

"A few minutes ago, I was riding the skateboard on my driveway when this big kid came running up the street and pushed me off the board. He took it and rode back the way he came." Leo pointed west down the street, the same direction Andrea and I had come from. "He skated off so fast and my knees were cut from the fall, I couldn't catch up to him."

"What did he look like?" I asked, wishing I had brought my notebook with me.

"I couldn't see his face," Leo sounded anxious. He was still pointing west toward the end of the street. "The sun was right behind him and blinded me. All I saw was his silhouette. He was big and had spiky hair. I think he went into the schoolyard."

"You better get yourself cleaned up, Leo," I said. His hands were covered in small cuts and his left arm was bruised. On his knees, two old scabs had been scraped off and were bleeding. "We'll take it from here."

"Forget it. It's gone," Leo said, already defeated.

"Don't be too sure," Andrea winked. "Lucky for you, Leo, I'm running with my very own detective."

School didn't start for another hour, but when we arrived, the steps outside the front door were already echoing with the sounds of skateboards slapping on rails and benches.

"Skaters here before school?"

There were six of them. Guys and girls. All too busy to notice two kids in running gear.

"You got to get out of bed earlier more often," Andrea grinned. "They're here every morning skating the rails until the caretaker shows up and chases them away."

I pointed to a big, spiky-haired teen who just landed a solid tailslide down a long handrail. Max would have been impressed. "He fits Leo's description."

"That's Austin," Andrea said in a hushed voice. "I heard he was banned from the local skate shop for shoplifting."

Austin didn't stop skating when we asked him about Leo.

"Yeah I know him," he answered between grinds. "Saw him skating in the street yesterday. We told him to be careful. Cars buzz down that street all the time. We heard a car screech and then him crying. By the time we got to the road, he was gone."

The school doors swung open. The sour-faced caretaker rushed out, shaking his fist. Austin and the other skaters were too fast. Within seconds, they were gone.

I turned back to the school gate, walking quickly toward Leo's house.

"Where you going?" Andrea asked. "Aren't you going to ask Austin more questions?"

"We don't have to. He didn't do it." I grinned, suddenly full of energy. Maybe this getting up early stuff wasn't so bad after all. "I know what happened to your board." **Do you know what happened to Andrea's skateboard? All the clues are here. Turn the page for the solution.**

Solution: The Case of the
Snatched Skateboard

Leo Ducharme.

Clues

* Alison spotted several mistakes in Leo's story about the skateboard thief. He pointed west when he was showing where the thief came from. He said the Sun was behind the thief, so he couldn't see his face. This is impossible. The Sun rises in the east, not the west.

* Leo said the thief pushed him down, cutting his knees. But the cuts had already formed a scab, which looked picked clean. That's because Leo got them the day before and made them bleed again to look like he'd been hurt that morning.

* Leo knew Andrea ran that route every morning. He timed his story so he'd run into her, but he wasn't expecting Alison to be there too. Leo said the skater rode off in the direction that Alison and Andrea had just come from.

If that was true, they would have seen the skater.

Conclusion

After Alison confronted Leo, he confessed to making up the story to hide what really happened. The day before, Leo was skating on the road and fell off his board, skinning his knees. The board rolled under the wheels of a passing car and snapped as the car screeched to a halt. Leo was terrified Andrea would make him pay for the broken board, so he made up the story of the thief. Leo felt so bad about lying, he gave Andrea money for the skateboard anyway.

Andrea bought new shoes and won the Whispering Meadows cross-country race for the fourth year in a row. Alison ran a great race, beat Max, and can now proudly claim to be the fastest detective in town.

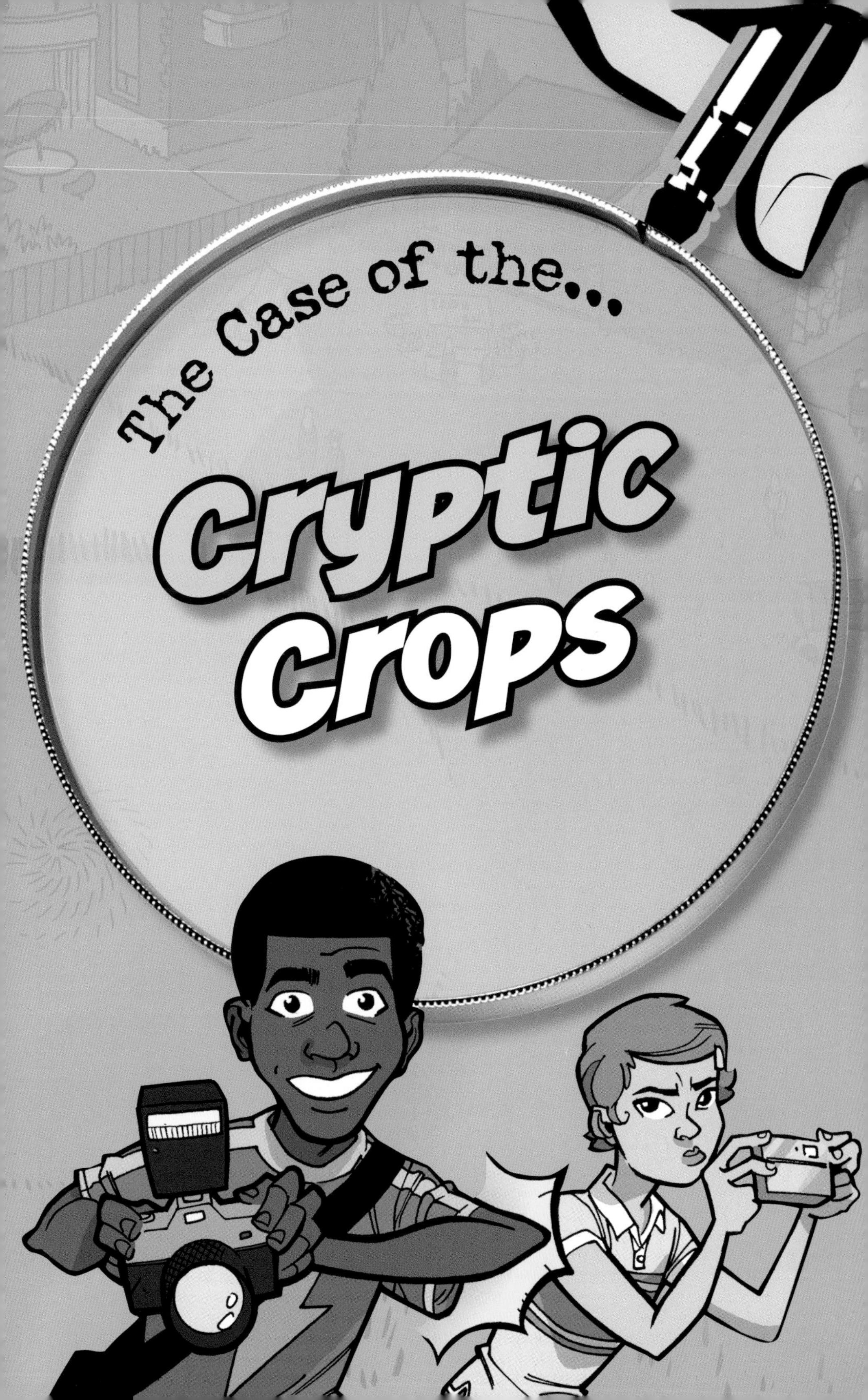
The Case of the...
Cryptic Crops

The Case of the Cryptic Crops

Max Finder here, junior high detective and super skeptic. When Alison told me she was taking pictures for the school paper of a UFO landing at our classmate Nicholas Musicco's farm, I had to tag along and check it out.

HEY NICHOLAS!

HEY GUYS, HURRY UP! COME GET A LOOK AT MY CROP CIRCLE.

CROP CIRCLE

FRESH CORN

ALIENS LANDING IN WHISPERING MEADOWS? I'LL BELIEVE IT WHEN I —

FRESH CORN

WHOA!

OUTTA THE WAY, GUYS. I GOT HERE FIRST, SO I GET THE SCOOP FOR THE SCHOOL PAPER.

BUMP

WHAT?! TAKING PICS FOR THE PAPER IS MY JOB!

Argh! Jake Granger was a classmate of ours and a thorn in my side. He barged ahead of us to interview Mr. Musicco, Nicholas's father.

SO, MR. MUSICCO, DID YOU NOTICE ANYTHING STRANGE LAST NIGHT?

IT WAS QUIET ALL NIGHT, BUT I SAW A MOVING LIGHT FROM MY BED. WHEN I GOT UP TO LOOK I DIDN'T SEE ANYTHING.

WILL YOU LOSE MUCH MONEY BECAUSE OF THE RUINED CROPS?

ACTUALLY, NO. IT WAS JUST A SMALL AMOUNT OF WHEAT. AND WE'RE DOING SO WELL AT THE PRODUCE STAND TODAY THAT WE'LL DEFINITELY MAKE THE MONEY BACK!

While Jake hogged the story, Alison and I took a closer look at the crop circle.

WHO COULD'VE DONE THIS? AND MORE IMPORTANTLY, WHY?

LOOK! THERE'S A HOLE IN THE CENTER OF THE CIRCLE. COULD BE EVIDENCE OF LANDING GEAR. I'LL CHECK IT OUT.

NOT SO FAST!

WHO ARE YOU?

SCULLY MULDER, GOVERNMENT *UFO* RESEARCHER. YOU WEREN'T TRYING TO DISTURB EVIDENCE, WERE YOU? THAT WOULD BE A CRIME.

FIRST, WE GET BEATEN TO THE PUNCH BY JAKE GRANGER. THEN WE'RE NEARLY ARRESTED BY THE *UFO* COPS. HAPPY NOW, ALISON? AL? HELLO?

I THINK I RECOGNIZE HER FROM THE NEWS...

Alison went to find a newspaper, so I talked to Nicholas.

SO DID *YOU* NOTICE ANYTHING WEIRD LAST NIGHT?

NOT A THING, AND I WAS CAMPING OUT IN THE BACKYARD! THOSE ALIENS MUST HAVE SOUND-DAMPENING TECHNOLOGY.

NICE SHIRT, NICHOLAS! YOU MUST HAVE *STYLE*-DAMPENING TECHNOLOGY.

WHAT'S HER PROBLEM?

THAT'S SASHA PRICE, MY NEXT-DOOR NEIGHBOR. HER FAMILY WANTS TO BUY OUR FARM AND PUT UP TENNIS COURTS.

LET'S GET OUT OF HERE. DID I TELL YOU ABOUT MY SHOPPING SPREE IN THE CITY? WE JUST GOT BACK THIS MORNING.

PSST! MAX!

I FOUND THIS IN THE MUSICCOS' RECYCLING BOX.

HEADLINE-HUNGRY UFO RESEARCHER DECLARED A FRAUD.

HMM, MAYBE SCULLY CREATED THE CROP CIRCLE TO GET HER NAME IN THE NEWS. LET'S DO SOME SNOOPING.

We looked around but found nothing that could be used to make a crop circle. Even worse, Scully drove off in a loud clunker before we could talk to her!

NOTHING IN HERE, EITHER.

BUT SOMETHING'S DEFINITELY HAPPENING OUT HERE, MAX.

WHAT'S UP WITH JAKE AND NICHOLAS?

COME ON, DETECTIVES. I'VE GOT A LEAD FOR YOU.

Jake led us to Sasha Price's yard.

NICHOLAS TOLD ME HE SAW SASHA DOING SOMETHING SUSPICIOUS IN HERE LAST NIGHT.

Aha!

WHAM!

We took the equipment out of the shed to test it.

WELL, I GUESS WE KNOW HOW THE CULPRIT CREATED THE CIRCLE.

AND I KNOW WHO MADE IT.

Do you know who is flattening the crops? All the clues are here. Turn the page for the solution.

Solution: The Case of the
Cryptic Crops

Who created the crop circles?
Nicholas Musicco.
He was worried about losing the land to Sasha Price and her family, so he made the crop circle to attract people to the farm.

How did he do it?
Nicholas created the circle using the tools Max, Alison, and Jake found. As Alison demonstrated, the board was used to flatten the crops. The spike was used to keep Nicholas moving around the center point in a perfect circle. After he was finished, he hid the tools in Sasha's shed to frame her.

Clues
* Mr. Musicco said the farm was making money selling produce.
* Scully Mulder drove a "loud clunker," but Mr. Musicco said it was a quiet night. That means she couldn't have driven up to the house to create the circle.
* Max didn't find any tools in Nicholas's tent, but he did notice a flashlight, which would explain why Mr. Musicco saw a "moving light" the night before.
* The running shoes on the floor of the tent were covered in wheat shafts.
* Nicholas told Jake that he saw Sasha moving around by her shed the night before, but she was in the city on a shopping spree. Nicholas was lying.

Conclusion
Nicholas admitted to creating the crop circle. His father made him put in extra time at the produce stand to make up for it, which was a good thing: even though the crop circle was an admitted fake, lots of people came to see it anyway -- and lots of them were hungry!

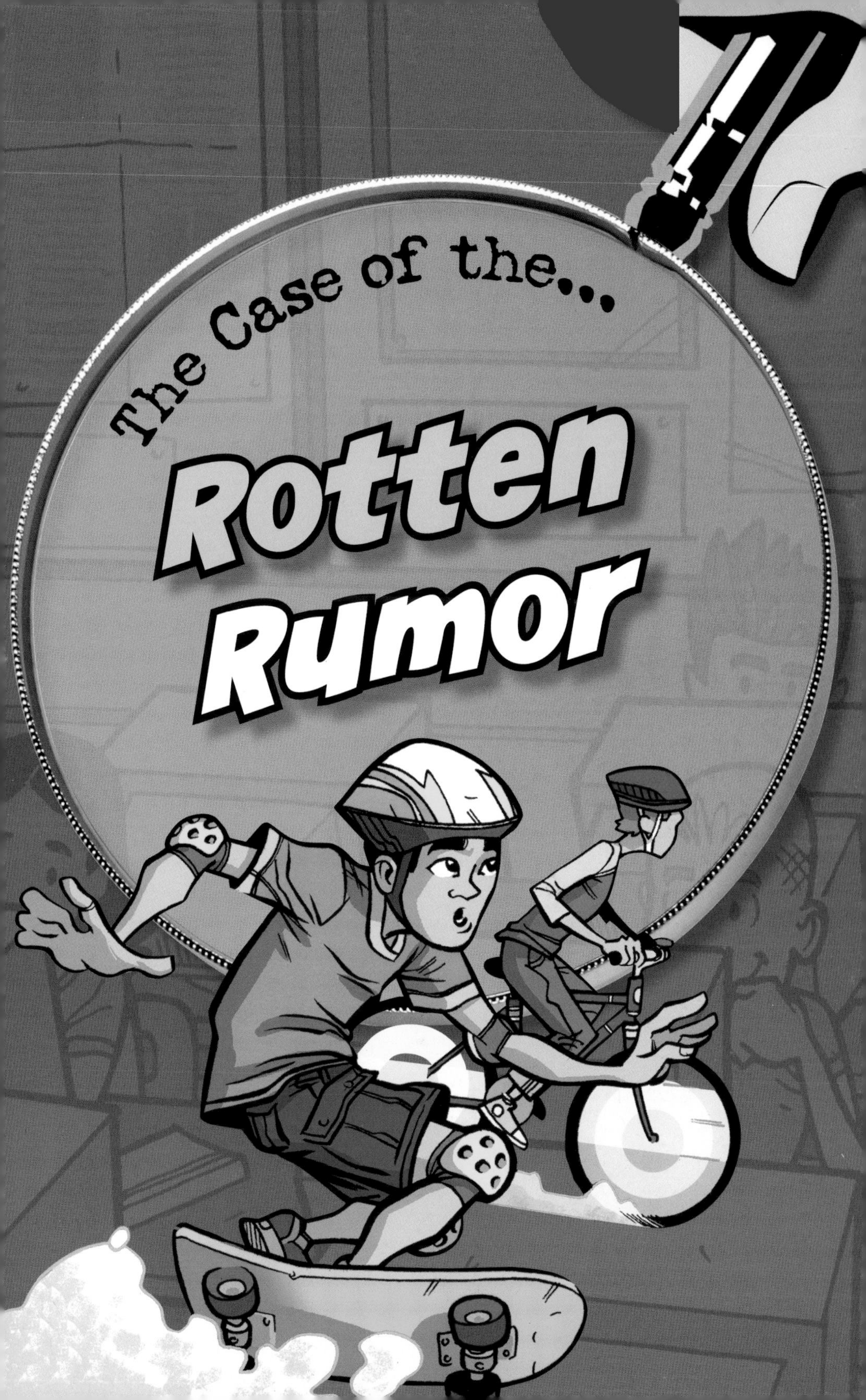
The Case of the...
Rotten Rumor

The Case of the Rotten Rumor

Max Finder here, junior high detective and weekend wanderer. Alison and I were taking a quiet ride through downtown Whispering Meadows one Sunday morning when...

EEK!

THAT SOUNDS LIKE JESSICA PEEVES!

LET'S CHECK IT OUT.

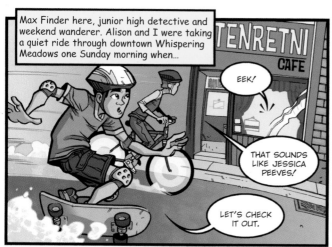

TELL ME WHO'S RESPONSIBLE FOR THIS!

IT'S NOT *MY* BLOG, MISS! I DON'T KNOW!

Jessica Peeves is known for wanting things her way, but not for freaking out on café employees. We calmed her down and tried to find out what was going on.

I JUST CHECKED *CMZ*, MY FAVE SCHOOL GOSSIP SITE. BUT *THAT* POST WAS UP THERE!

WHAT POST?

CMZ CENTRAL MEADOWS ZONE!

| HOME | CMZ TV | PHOTOS | VIDEOS | CMZ MOBILE |

PEEVED AT PEEVES
Here's something you didn't know about Jessica Peeves, courtesy of an anonymous tip.
She PAYS her way onto school clubs and sports teams. In fact, she paid $100 to get a spot on the track team. Maybe she should change her name to "Jessica BRIBES."

Posted at 11:17 by hckstr

I MADE THE TEAM FAIR AND SQUARE!

SHE'S TELLING THE TRUTH, MAX. SHE'S REALLY FAST. I SAW HER AT TRYOUTS WHILE I WAS TAKING PICTURES FOR THE NEWSPAPER.

SO SOMEONE STARTED A RUMOR. IT'S UP TO US TO FIND OUT WHO.

Jessica took off for home, dreading the thought of showing her face at school the next day. But Leslie Chang wasn't sympathizing.

IF SHE'S SO UPSET, SHE SHOULD JUST GET HER RICH DAD TO BUY THE INTERNET.

OKAY, SHERLOCK. *CMZ* IS ALL ABOUT OUR SCHOOL, SO WE KNOW THE BLOGGER'S A CLASSMATE. BUT HOW DO WE SOLVE A CRIME WITHOUT A CRIME SCENE?

ELEMENTARY, MY DEAR ALISON. WE CALL IN SOME HELP.

Our friend Zoe is an expert in forensics and a computer whiz. She also loves helping us solve mysteries.

MAX! I DID THE RESEARCH YOU ASKED FOR!

THE BLOG WAS POSTED AT *11:17* AM BY SOMEONE NAMED "HCKSTR."

"HACK STAR"? "HUCKSTER"? THAT'S NOT MUCH TO GO ON.

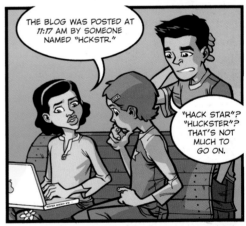

I TRIED TO TRACE THE BLOGGER, BUT THE SITE ROUTES TRAFFIC THROUGH AN OVERLAY NETWORK AND HIDES THE IP ADDRESS.

MY HEAD HURTS. CAN YOU SAY THAT AGAIN IN ENGLISH?

IT'S COMPLETELY ANONYMOUS, MAX. WE'RE BACK TO SQUARE ONE.

It was obvious at school the next day that Alison, Zoe, and I weren't the only ones reading CMZ on Sunday afternoon.

IT MUST'VE COST JESSICA A FORTUNE TO GET TO THE TOP OF THE *P.A.S.S.* CHART!

P.A.S.S. stands for Participation, Activity, Study, and Sport. You earn points for joining clubs and playing on teams. Jessica claimed the top spot when she made the track team.

I KNEW IT! EVERYONE THINKS I'M A CHEATER.

DON'T WORRY, JESSICA. LAY LOW FOR A WHILE, AND WE'LL GET TO THE BOTTOM OF THIS.

We started with Tony DeMatteo. He's the best hockey player in town — and Jessica's biggest competition for the top P.A.S.S. spot.

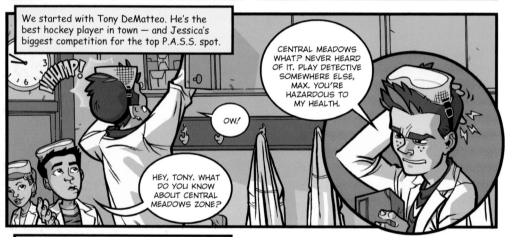

WHUMP!

OW!

HEY, TONY. WHAT DO YOU KNOW ABOUT CENTRAL MEADOWS ZONE?

CENTRAL MEADOWS WHAT? NEVER HEARD OF IT. PLAY DETECTIVE SOMEWHERE ELSE, MAX. YOU'RE HAZARDOUS TO MY HEALTH.

Leslie said she didn't know who the blogger was either. But she told us Jessica had replaced Zoe's sister, Andrea Palgrave, on the track squad.

IT'S TRUE. I SAW THE TEAM ROSTER MYSELF.

THAT GIVES ANDREA A MOTIVE, AND I HATE TO SAY IT, BUT ZOE'S COMPUTER SKILLS WOULD MAKE HER A GREAT ACCOMPLICE.

THANKS, LESLIE. HEY, DID YOU HEAR THAT THE BAND MONKEY'S JUNKYARD IS PLAYING A CONCERT HERE NEXT MONTH?

SERIOUSLY? THAT'S AWESOME!

UH, WHEN DID YOU START SPREADING RUMORS, MAX?

YOU KNOW WHAT THEY SAY, ALISON. IF YOU CAN'T BEAT 'EM... JOIN 'EM.

IF ANYONE HAS ANY QUESTIONS ABOUT THE ASSIGNMENT, PLEASE COME SEE ME NOW. MS. PALGRAVE! YOU'RE LATE!

SORRY, MR. BISSELL.

TD IS A HOCKEY STAR!

HERE COMES ANDREA.

A few minutes into class, Alison got my attention.

PSST, MAX! CHECK THE BLOG!

IT WORKED, ALISON! MY FAKE NEWS MADE THE SITE.

DOES THAT MEAN "HCKSTR" IS IN THIS CLASS?

YES, AND I THINK THE UNDERCOVER BLOGGER IS ABOUT TO BE EXPOSED.

Do you know who "hckstr" is? All the clues are here. Turn the page for the solution.

Solution: The Case of the
Rotten Rumor

Who started the rumor?

Tony DeMatteo.

It's no secret he's a fierce competitor, and he didn't like being so close to the top of the P.A.S.S. chart without being in the lead. He used his gossip blog to ruin Jessica's reputation.

Clues

* When Max and Alison asked Tony about the blog, he said he'd never heard of it. Still, he had the initials "CMZ" written on his binder when he walked into the computer lab.

* Max noticed Leslie whispering something to Tony before computer class. She was telling him the news about the Monkey's Junkyard concert.

* Leslie was at the front of the classroom at the time the Monkey's Junkyard post went live.

* On the chalkboard in the computer class it says, "TD is a hockey star." Max noticed this, and the name of the blogger became clear: "TD" stands for Tony Dematteo, and "hckstr" is short for "hockey star."

* Andrea Palgrave had a cast on her ankle when she walked into class. That's why she was replaced on the track team. She'd have no reason to be jealous of Jessica.

Conclusion

When Max presented his evidence and threatened to check the history of Tony's computer in the lab, Tony finally confessed to keeping the blog. He apologized to Jessica, but she didn't even seem all that mad. She said it was understandable that people would be jealous of her success!

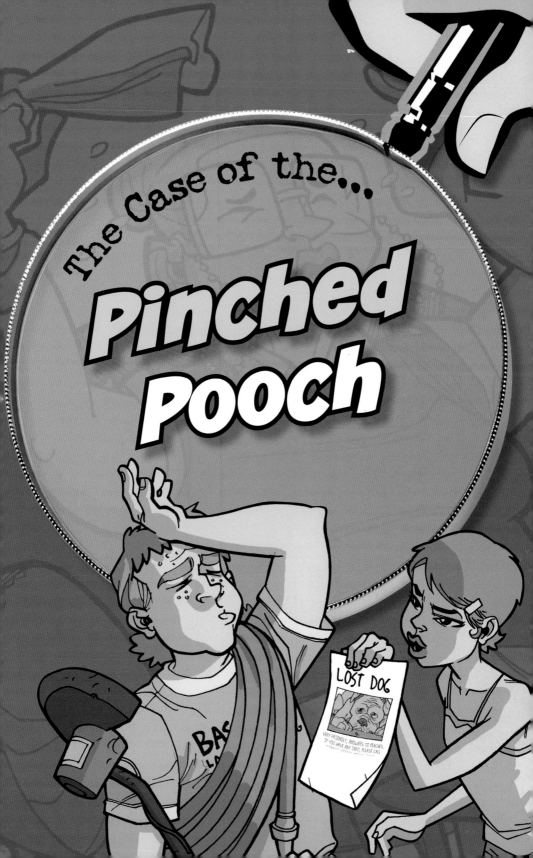

The Case of the
Pinched Pooch

Max Finder here, junior high detective and reluctant lawn mower. Luckily, I've always got my best friend Alison around to distract me from my chores.

HEY MAX! THERE'S A MYSTERY RIGHT IN YOUR BACKYARD — LITERALLY!

OOF.

LOST DOG

VERY FRIENDLY, ANSWERS TO PEACHES. IF YOU HAVE ANY INFO, PLEASE CALL ELEANOR BRIGGS AT 555-7909.

WHAT DO YOU THINK?

I THINK THE LAWN CAN WAIT. LET'S GO TALK TO MRS. BRIGGS.

Mrs. Briggs lives in the house just behind mine. Her dog, Peaches, is the most pampered pup in Whispering Meadows. He's also the best barker on the block.

WHERE WERE YOU WHEN PEACHES WENT MISSING?

WELL, AS YOU CAN SEE, I HAVEN'T BEEN FEELING VERY WELL...

I don't like leaving Peaches cooped up, but I'm in no shape to walk him. Crystal Diallo was supposed to take him in the afternoon, but she never showed up.

I let Peaches down into the yard for a couple of hours while I took an afternoon nap. When I woke up, he was gone!

DID YOU NOTICE ANYONE IN THE BACK ALLEY WHEN YOU WERE ON YOUR BALCONY?

NO! IT WAS JUST PEACHES AND ME OUT BACK ALL MORNING.

We headed to the backyard to comb the crime scene. It took Zoe, our friend and forensics expert, all of five minutes to find a clue.

GUYS! CHECK IT OUT.

IT'S A PIECE OF GREEN COTTON FABRIC, POSSIBLY FROM A T-SHIRT. IT MIGHT BE NOTHING...

SURE, ZOE. BUT IT COULD BE EVERYTHING.

LET'S GO SEE IF MRS. BRIGGS RECOGNIZES —

WHAM!

Russell Wagner's family shares a fence with Mrs. Briggs. He doesn't like Peaches's barking, and doesn't care who knows it.

TAKE IT EASY, RUSSELL! YOU SHOOK THE WHOLE FENCE.

MAYBE THAT'LL SCARE SOME SENSE INTO THAT DUMB DOG OVER THERE.

THAT "DUMB DOG" IS MISSING. KNOW ANYTHING ABOUT THAT?

TALK TO CRYSTAL DIALLO. I SAW HER WITH THE DOG YESTERDAY AFTERNOON, AND SHE LOOKED EVEN MADDER THAN ME.

Around the block, we saw Crystal and she told us she did walk Peaches yesterday. Mrs. Briggs didn't answer the door, so Crystal got him from the backyard.

I CAUGHT MY SHIRT ON THE LATCH WHEN I DROPPED PEACHES OFF — A PIECE OF IT WAS STUCK THERE WHEN I LEFT. I WAS FURIOUS!

HAVE YOU TALKED TO BASHER? HE AND HIS STEPBROTHER, STUART DESILVA, MOW MRS. BRIGGS'S LAWN.

BRAINS + BRAWN
BASHER BRO
~Lawn Mowing
call 555-2510

HMM. YOUR LAWN COULD USE A TRIM, COULDN'T IT, MAX?

Ben "Basher" McGintley is better known for his stomach-punching than his landscaping. Alison called him and said we had a lawn emergency.

OH NO, NOT THE DORK-TECTIVES!

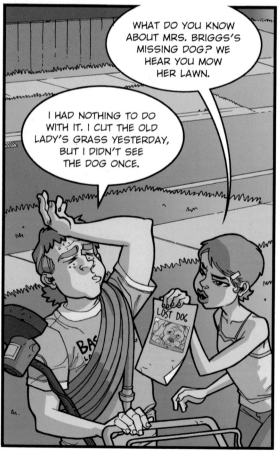

WHAT DO YOU KNOW ABOUT MRS. BRIGGS'S MISSING DOG? WE HEAR YOU MOW HER LAWN.

I HAD NOTHING TO DO WITH IT. I CUT THE OLD LADY'S GRASS YESTERDAY, BUT I DIDN'T SEE THE DOG ONCE.

LOST DOG

SINCE WHEN DO YOU MOW LAWNS, BASHER?

SINCE I DECIDED TO BUY A NEW MOUNTAIN BIKE. IT'S GONNA COST ME $500. HEY, YOU NEED THESE HEDGES TRIMMED? ONLY AN EXTRA FIVE BUCKS!

After Basher finished up, we walked over to the dog park to ask some questions. Nobody had kind things to say about Crystal.

SHE'S ALWAYS LATE PICKING UP THE DOGS. BUT I THINK I SAW THIS DOG WITH A KID OVER BY THE FOREST.

THERE'S PEACHES!

HEY!

HURRY, MAX! THEY'VE DISAPPEARED INTO THE WOODS.

WE LOST THEM. I DIDN'T EVEN GET A GOOD LOOK.

I, ON THE OTHER HAND, HAVE SEEN ENOUGH. I KNOW WHO STOLE PEACHES.

REWARD

Do you know who pinched Mrs. Briggs's dog? All the clues are here. Turn the page for the solution.

Solution: The Case of the
Pinched Pooch

Who stole Peaches?

Basher McGintley — with the help of his stepbrother, Stuart. Basher needed $500 to pay for a new mountain bike, and he kidnapped Peaches in order to claim reward money.

Clues

* Mrs. Briggs said she slept for a couple of hours. That left lots of time for Crystal to walk Peaches and return him, and for Basher to swoop in and steal him.

* Crystal said a bit of her shirt got stuck on the fence, but Zoe found it on the ground. That means someone knocked the fabric off after she left. It was Basher.

* Basher said he mowed Mrs. Briggs's lawn on the day of the theft, but the lawn didn't look freshly mowed.

* When Basher came by Max's house, he was struggling with his equipment. That's because Stuart usually helps him out.

Stuart was busy looking after Peaches.

* The woman in the park said Crystal has a bad reputation for showing up late. This explains why she didn't arrive at Mrs. Briggs's on time to walk Peaches.

* Basher and Stuart were both wearing blue work shirts in the "Basher Bros. Lawn Mowing" poster. Max noticed the thief in the park was wearing a blue shirt under his sweatshirt. It was Stuart.

* After the chase, Max noticed that the "Lost Dog" poster on the lamppost had a new headline: "Reward." That's when it all became clear.

Conclusion

When Max and Alison presented their evidence, Basher confessed to stealing Peaches. He returned the prized pup and promised to mow Mrs. Briggs's lawn for free for the rest of the summer.

Meet the Creators

Liam O'Donnell

Liam O'Donnell is the author of many children's books and the creator of *Max Finder Mystery* and the *Graphic Guide Adventures* series of graphic novels. In addition to writing for kids, Liam teaches Grade 1, plays video games and goes camping (but not all at the same time.) He lives in Toronto, Canada. You can visit him online at **liamodonnell.com**

Meet the Creators

Craig Battle

Craig Battle grew up in Lantzville, British Columbia, and honed his writing skills at the University of Victoria. Craig's previous job titles include reporter, camp counselor, and basketball coach, but he has been editor of *OWL Magazine* since 2006. *Max Finder Mystery* is the first comic Craig's ever written that doesn't star himself. You can read his blog at **www.owlkids.com/owlblog**.

Ramón Pérez

Ramón Pérez has been enjoying the life of a cartoonist for longer than he can remember, with a catalogue of work as diverse as the styles he employs. His repertoire includes comic books, graphic novels, children's books, character design, magazines, and whatever else crosses his path that intrigues him!